THE DOUBTS OF ST. THOMAS

THE DOUBTS OF ST. THOMAS

Lt. SanTommaso

Emanuel C. Marchese

thank you
Margeull

iUniverse, Inc.

New York Lincoln Shanghai

THE DOUBTS OF ST. THOMAS
Lt. SanTommaso

iUniverse books may be ordered through booksellers or by contacting:

iUniverse
2021 Pine Lake Road, Suite 100
Lincoln, NE 68512
www.iuniverse.com
1-800-Authors (1-800-288-4677)

ISBN-13: 978-0-595-35111-4 (pbk)
ISBN-13: 978-0-595-79813-1 (ebk)
ISBN-10: 0-595-35111-5 (pbk)
ISBN-10: 0-595-79813-6 (ebk)

Printed in the United States of America

Free of all nonsense and Glory,
his job, for whatever it was worth, *is* his Glory!

CHAPTER 1

▼

Tommaso SanTommaso, his American acquired name, 'Tom St. Thomas', had just returned from a quick trip to his hometown, Melilli, Sicily. Built on two plateaus on one of the chains of the *Monti Iblei*, the inhabitants went proud of their town's large territory. It stretched up to the threshold of surrounding neighborly towns and the Province where two Malls were built on its footsteps.

Along the niches of the slopes, old and new villas and houses hung before the tableland.

SanTommaso's house stood in a split-level style with two entrances: one, the casual or familiar entrance with access to the ground floor from a narrow street below. The other, on the first floor from the above street, was the main, indeed, the guests' entrance, which meant an extra five minutes of climbing for visitors. To ascend the residence through narrow streets and endless flight of steps, it could initiate an asthmatic disorder for anybody passed the age of ten. As a young man, SanTommaso spent a lot of time in the upper level where the bedrooms, living room, a small library and the balconies were. After school and after a quick bite, he sat on the balcony reading and studying, unless his friends didn't whistle from the below ground; a signal that it was time to hit town and mingle with other boys for bullying of all sorts. They were good boys but still boys. At times the bullying would carry on too long affecting the wrong people. Sensitive people that along the way in life had forgotten humor, experiencing loss of energy or simply with the approach of old age had become miserable. That reminded Tommaso of his aged schoolteacher Miss. Monero, saying, "one doesn't become miserable with age, one has to be born miserable." Of course, his teacher's saying was not enough to keep him out of trouble with the local authorities and especially with the Carabinieri, which caused friction with his father, whose tendencies were of strict nature. But when he sat on the balcony reading or studying and his friends didn't whistle from the street below, he felt grownup. At times, he would lift his head from the books. He stretched his eyes eastwardly remaining enchanted by the panoramic views.

And he was not the only one.

The dazzling colors of the Ionian Sea would take the breath away. Mount Etna, northward, stood 'sempre eterna' against time, which superbly and invulnerably dominated the whole island, showing off its snow pinnacle in the winter and the greenery spotted with aridness in the summer. A daily spectacle of those who sat on a balcony of their own residence or walked along the town garden or sat on one of its wrought iron benches.

On clear days, which were many all throughout the year, the view extended further to the bottom of the peninsula's Apennines Chain. The antecedently mentioned Ionian, with its celebrated shores and beaches together with the peninsula's seas, the Tyrrhenian and the Adriatic, contributes fame to the whole Mediterranean Sea.

Tom was on his way to Hartford. His arrival, at Kennedy International under one of the worst snowstorms of the century, was delayed for the better part of two hours. Already tipsy for the ten-hour flight had taken thirteen hours, his bent attitude was reaching moments of despair. And the despair could have been somehow mitigated if the endless lines behind the cubicles of the Custom House moved faster.

He stalled. He sighed.

"Why in hell all the planes from Europe have to land at the same horrendous moment." Signs of irascibility were flickering in his head.

Lost in the track of time, all of a sweat, he became irascible. He longed for a smoke. At last his turn came. He turned in his passport.

Detective lieutenant Tommaso Santommaso, whose eyes were trained to see farther, always focused and instantly capable of memorizing numbers, faces, facts, were blinded by an inner furor. He had not noticed the attendant was a she-officer.

"If she's PM-assing I'm fucked." He quickly thought as he become conscious of it.

"Please open your suitcase!" she arrogantly asked as if she'd heard him.

"The audacity this fucking bitch..." he murmured loud enough to confusedly reach her ears.

"Excuse me?"

"I said...with all the fucking chaos..." he quickly bit on his lips for repeating the four letter word, albeit in combination with chaos instead of bitch this time. "I am an officer of the law...I am a cop; lieutenant Tom St. Thomas." he said fuming. And one could see the fumes coming out of his ears and nostrils.

"It's the law, lieutenant sir! You ought to know that." she said with arrogance an audacity. "Please open the suitcase."

"It's the law!" he hated that expression, especially coming from a woman. In the seventies, during the famous rather infamous shortage of gasoline, his car ran out of gas at a station seven miles from Hartford. He used up all of his learned kind words to convince the bitch that just a gallon was all he needed to get home.

The day fell on an even day, his date of birth fell on an odd day.

One must assume luck had been on his side on other unpredictable times. Running out of gas during that horrendous time had become a weekly routine, for Thomas' mind navigated more about the incompetence of the politicians not being able to foresee its coming. The reality was that he was stuck with that dilemma, like everybody else.

"It's the law!" she had repeated over and over with unrealistic pique and only to prove a point that she was in command.

God forgive some little trashy people that when given a little position of command, exercise it with the power of arrogance.

He stepped out. He took a deep breath and promised himself again to strengthen the effort to calm down.

"So? No big deal! I've been in worse situations!"

Undetermined hours of dangerous and miserable driving were ahead of him under the present circumstance. However, calmly and astonishingly so, totally in contrast with his wretched disposition, he smiled. He turned his back to the wind and lit a cigarette. He dragged it deeply and exhaled the puffs powerfully. He smoked it to the bitter end. He smiled wisely and uttered, *"Dulcis in fundo!"* A Latin expression meaning, 'Sweet at the end', which was customary of him to say in many occasions when related to the end of things. And, of course, his saying *"Dulcis in fundo"* (sweet at the end) alluded also and often to the act of fellatio and cunnilingus.

The cigarette did the job. He was calm and ready to cross the perverse and long tract of heavy snow that led to his car. He sunk his feet on the snow with the same grace and faithfulness as an Eskimo sinks his. He reached the long-term parking lot.

His Alfa Romeo spider veloce convertible was nowhere in sight.

It seemed to be hibernating under a blanket of snow.

"I'd like to know," he murmured. He didn't say further. He remembered he had made a wish to take it easy, as easy as one could under the present circumstances.

There was nobody around. Not one single nut other than himself, wacky enough, to attempt the drama to find a car that had basically vanished. The numbers on the posted signs that delineated the checkered parking spaces, the only beacon that could lead to the burial, were also heavily powdered. The snow would have probably melted and cleared the signs the next day if the upcoming chills weren't announcing subzero temperature.

He took a long glance over the dazzling white plateau and smiled. There was nothing to smile about but his determination that when things were beyond control, balance if not harmony takes place and discomforts ought to be mitigated by the way of thinking positive.

Disoriented and drenched to the bones, with his shoes looking more like Indian moccasins than Bruno Magli loafers, he attempted the return to the terminal. He made it, albeit he didn't believe it possible. Then drifting inside he stepped directly to the car-rental-counter and with tolerant civilization, stood in line. And all observed silence as if standing in line before paying the last respect to a deceased best friend in a Funeral Home.

He looked at those people with wonder. How civilized everyone was. But mostly it was the silence that impressed him.

"In my country," he thought, "The shouts would have reached deafening apocalyptic dimensions."

And as in a Funeral Home people moved quietly smooth.

He was soon second in line.

"Not a chance! Not until Saturday!" proffered the attendant with droopy eyes to the man in front of him.

"That's three days…from now…unbelievable! Can you believe that?"

"And you must reserve it now!" the attendant with droopy eyes vaguely stated.

"What are the odds for a room at the Hilton or a room anywhere that I can walk to?" the passenger retorted.

The man with droopy eyes attempted a smile. Then he just said, "Are you a comedian?"

The man furiously left the post vacant.

The attendant distractedly threw a droopy glance at Tom.

"Now what can I do for you?"

"Nothing! Thank you!"

He drifted off.

Outside the main door, the forewarning blizzard infuriated tortuously and gave rise to a play of glacial whiffs that took his breath away. Quick in reflexes and instinct, he raised both palms to his face to shield it and prevent the chafing from the insisting whirl of loose tiny pieces of flying ice crystal. As a last moment resolve and with eyes half closed, he looked around before returning to the terminal.

Perhaps he might catch a cab, a bus, a limo, or even a bike that would give him a lift to Hartford.

All means of transportation were booked and there was no bike in sight.

"Why am I in this chaos?" His inner voice told him! "No way I can take this bullshit any longer!"

Cold and shivering, still covering his face with both palms, he returned inside. He shook his snow dust from his clothes like a dog shakes dirt from its coat and then looked all around for a seat. An unoccupied and forgotten seat in a forgotten corner flared in his eyes. He rushed his steps and quickly sat. Tom took his loafers off and pulled his wet socks off. He subsided into the chair the best he could and minutes later he slumbered.

To sleep or not to sleep, that's the dilemma, to say it in the style of the great William.

He skated his butt from corner to corner within the perimeter of the seat. The armrests insisted on digging into his ribs, mitigating or alternating the soreness. He then had this inkling that the bullshit he found himself immersed in was of another day.

His cell shrilled. The Caller ID showed Maria's number, his eternal girlfriend. He hesitated to answer. He wasn't sure. Will talking to her, will it alleviate or aggravate his disposition?

"Where are you?" She asked worried as he opened the communication.

"Stranded! I'm stranded for the night or maybe days! I'm dozing on a fucking uncomfortable chair in the fucking terminal! I can't get my car out. I don't even know under which slab of ice it is hiding…"

"I'll come pick you up!"

"Don't you fuck move! You come and pick me up? What're you crazy! That's all I need is worrying about you getting killed. Besides, the access to Long Island is impossible; every fucking bridge is jammed with traffic."

"Why all those four letter words when he spoke to Maria if his previous disposition was somehow under control?" He asked himself.

"I'm moving to Florida! Are you coming?"

"That's new yet!"

"It's not new at all! Has been in my head since I was born…"

"Thank you for sharing it with me."

"Maria, are you going to nag me?"

"I didn't mean to, I'm sorry!"

"It's not real…I cannot have a decent fight with this woman…it would clean up the bad blood in my brain…she's not normal!" he thought attempting a smile that never rose to his lips. "Okay, listen! I'll call you first thing tomorrow morning. Get a goodnight sleep! I love you!" And click!

As he shut the phone he poetically recited, "Hartford, my beautiful! I love you too! But your atmospheric caprices remind me of the roller-coaster temperament of beautiful women! And I had it with you…and with beautiful women!"

But Maria…although beautiful she's quiet leveled. Am I lucky of what? Or is a dream that I'm dreaming?"

Moving? It was easy to say! What about his job? Hartford was his livelihood. Lieutenant Thomas St. Thomas was an assistant there of the Crime Investigation Bureau. Furthermore his promotion to take full charge of the Bureau was at hand.

Maria's livelihood didn't matter! Her curriculum vitae spoke so loud that a job was probably already waiting for her in Florida or anywhere in the country.

An ironic smile surfaced his lips for that uncomfortable chair could not be abandoned; even for a quick visit to the men's room. And he had to take a leak so badly his bladder ached. But even taking a few steps around it to remove the armrests from his ribs meant to say goodbye to his seat for the remaining hours of the night.

The other passengers that like him were stranded and stood in groups in every corner, or sat on their suitcases, or lay on the floor resting their heads on the handbag, would indecently dive on it. Or in a civilized manner, if at all possible, pay an unreasonable amount of money to occupy it. Any chair!

The thought to relocate to Florida grew as the crack of dawn drew nearer. And the more he looked at the people around him, spaced out people as if overdosed from an unsuspected use of illicit drug, the more the idea to move to Florida appealed to him.

At times, all through the night, he talked to himself.

"Why in hell did I go home for?"

Home was no longer the same place of old?

He went back home every few years to renew his identity, his national foibles, and the craziness that surrounded them all. Because most of all, albeit he had embraced the American ways, he was an Italian, even worse a Sicilian. However, there were certain things about being Sicilian that appealed to him. Perhaps that hot temper that made them burst for very little, but cooled so fast one never knew it had happened. Arrogance and virility, they felt handsome even if they were not; sure with the opposite sex.

This time he was disappointed and his attitude towards the Sicilian men and of course, women had changed; at least for the time being. The truth was that his parents were now dead and some of his closest friends either were also dead, or downrightly lived in other cities or other states.

Forget it! Forget about hometown! Florida was his new alternative. Furthermore, Florida is a state with beauty of its own and the weather? You can't beat the weather! In a way it would be like living back home for the mild tempered winter of the peninsula reminded him of his beloved Island.

While on the bus the following thought took him to Hartford with a quick stop in New Haven for the discharge of some passengers. He wrote down the itinerary for the moving. Although doubts of every kind were part of his daily living, he impulsively, as he had done years back when choosing to immigrate to the United States, he chose to move to Florida.

"Florida will be my final residence!" Final because Florida offered warm weather, and that he wanted, and perhaps, also final, if one considered the dangerous nature of the job. Life was at risk on a daily basis in his line of work.

One year passed before the opening in Florida for the position he longed for. Lieutenant St. Thomas, without hesitation whatsoever, applied for it and got accepted as head crime investigator. He would be under the existing commander of the Bureau, Capt. Robert Baker, in the city of BB between Boca Raton and Palm Beach.

At first Maria was reluctant to follow him. She loved him. She loved him unconditionally. Accepted! She had accepted all since the very beginning of their relationship even his peculiarities, his foibles and even his sarcasm!

But because of his insecurities and doubts she made one single but undisputed request: rent her own apartment. At least until he was totally ready for the celebrated, assumingly forever, commitment, 'Marriage.'

CHAPTER 2

▼

Five days had passed since Tom sat on a comfortable chair in his brand new office. From time to time he caressed the shining and glaring finish of the wood while reading the curriculum vitae of his assigned detectives. He needed to know of what kind of paste they were made of.

Three murder cases within his jurisdiction shook him up from his lethargic state. "Sonofabitch! Why not one per each town? Why all on me at this early moment of my career?" he muttered to himself. Nothing yet! He knew nothing about his helpers and their mental capacity. Why if they were incompetent? And all investigations with all the massive work that goes with it will fall solely on his shoulders; the bullshit, the captain with his certain air of command, and the chief's nonsense.

Suddenly, Tommaso SanTommaso stopped caressing the shining and glaring desk with the palm of his hand. He stood up and paced the floor for an indeterminate length of time. Likewise, outside the office, his assigned senior detective Sergeant Dan Macday, also paced the floor. Dan debated if knocking at the door was, at that particular early hour of the morning, inconvenient. The quickness of the set of circumstances seized the small team into an uncomfortable, eerie, and frightening frenzy. Within the framework of three hours, three brutal murders had been committed a few miles away from each other.

St. Thomas paged Loren Duster, a pretty young officer whose functions were those of a coordinator and a secretary. She sat at a desk located in a vital corner of a large lobby facing the offices of the chief, the captain and the lieutenant. She splendidly took care of their needs but her major assignment was to look after her new boss, Lieutenant SanTommaso and his investigators. Loren startled at the sound of the voice. She was making rhythmical nervous movements with her hands while shuffling a deck of cards. She waited patiently for Tom to throw on her desk the necessary paperwork to start the ball rolling. Amid shuffling the cards she would at intervals roll her eyes at Dan. He never missed an opportunity to roll his eyes back at her while pacing the floor in front of the office, albeit absorbed with doubt, pity, and a bunch of other emotions.

"Tell Dan to come in!"

"Yes sir! Anything else?"

"Yeah, ask him to bring me a fucking cup of coffee…"

"Regular?"

"Does it really matter?"

"No! Sir! Right away!"

"Why are you standing at the door as if you had a death in your family?" he asked Dan, barely controlling his temper.

Dan, still hesitant, stood on his six-feet-four frame with a cup of coffee totally eclipsed by his enormous hand. Then he smiled a shy smile as he forwarded his first gigantic step.

"How many detectives beside you, do we have in our unit?" he asked as if he didn't know.

"Two! Met them, you know! Phil Donahue and Jim Casa."

"Do you expect me to remember all the names at once?" he said as if in charge of an Army Corps. "I'm only sitting at this fucking desk five days…at any rate did the coroner release any information yet, find anything we can go with, other than information inside this manila envelope which says less than nothing?" he asked in one single breath. Then he added, "If less than nothing was at all possible!" And with that he put the cup of coffee that Dan handed him on top of the manila and lit a cigarette.

"No sir! He did not!"

"No sir?"

"No!"

The cigarette puffs blown out of his mouth and nostrils channeled the air in slow serpentine motion. The escaping smoke out of the cup of coffee also glided in the air drawing closer to the other smoke. Then as a faded dancing silhouette it zigzagged away.

Dan noticed he never took a sip of coffee out of that cup. Perhaps he has other hairs to pull off his ass. Dan also noticed he looked stressed out. Lieutenant St. Thomas was new at the job. It was so essential to prove himself worthy of the position.

"Show me your ass and I'll burn it," he murmured, thinking of the killer or killers.

"Sorry lieutenant, I didn't hear you."

"Never mind! Do you know Gianni Russo personally?"

"Sure do! He's a new kid but sharp as a razor and funny. Hell if he's funny!"

"…Funny?" Tom murmured. He didn't find him funny when he gave him a speeding citation.

Almost daily, time and weather permitting, Tom liked to take a spin with his Alfa Romeo. A mind liberating obligation that mitigated the daily stress under which his job obliged him. Top down, for an hour or so he sped along I-95 either southbound or north, depending solely on his moods. The benefit derived from that driving was overwhelming. However, he sincerely believed that it was solely to benefit the car: allow its carburetor, 'lungs' he called it, to breath. That day the choice fell on South Beach. Drive along the avenue and maybe time permitting, take a seat in one of those tiny cafes for a beer or two.

He furiously took Boynton Beach Gateway exit raising his MPH on the speedometer to seventy on a thirty-five speed limit zone. As he entered the highway, he zagged the lines of cars at 90. Just as he passed Woolbright exit he heard the motorbike's siren.

Of course, he pulled over.

The cop approached him nonchalantly.

"License and registration, please!" Then he looked at the belt still in its usual standing position, and asked, "Is there any reason why you're not buckled up?"

"Sure," Tom said smiling arrogantly. "I've just unbuckled as I heard the siren!"

The cop nodded his head. He read the license as it was handed to him and read the mandatory building security card still pinned on the lapel of his jacket: Lt. T. SanTommaso. Again he nodded his head and mumbled, "Uh uh, Lieutenant...Lieutenant SanTommaso!" Are you aware you were going 30 miles, zigzag fashion, in excess of the posted limit?

"If you say so?"

"I say so! Better yet my laser says so! Please remain inside!" he said. Then he walked to his car for the routinely inspection and to write the citation.

Tom was fuming but managed to control himself without ostentation. He wanted to justify the fact that the cop was just doing his duty.

When the officer returned with charges of speed plus the forty-seven dollars for not being strapped, the cup hath runeth over two hundred.

"Almost fucking three hundred!" he murmured. He didn't think that young sonofabitch would have the audacity to fine his superior in rank.

No complaints. The sonofabitch was being meticulous in his line of work. However, in accordance with his character, Tom had to have his two cents in, thus as he read the officer's name on his pocket lapel, he asked.

"Officer Russo, what the initial G stands for?"

"Gianni, sir! Gianni Russo!"

"Then, while smiling sarcastically, he looked deeply into the young cop's eyes and said, "For what I can see at this point in time it seems you're going to give speeding tickets for the rest of your brilliant career!"

"Not at all sir. Only at this point in time." he smiled. "My goal is to go on with all the career's opportunity the agency has to offer. I'll take advantage of every opportunity."

He said it so arrogantly Tom saw himself in the young officer.

The balls on that punk! He should have at least mitigated the price of the fine.

Another motorist passed by in excess of the posted speed limit.

"Have a good day lieutenant Sir! I must go!"

Thus he ran over and jumped on his bike. He spun it around on its pedal and chased the new offender.

"Fucking punk!" Tom murmured.

"So?" Tom said to Dan snapping out of the trance.

"So what sir?"

"What do you think about it?"

"About what sir?"

"Weren't we talking about Gianni Russo?" he asked and flapped the palm of his hand on his forehead.

"I told you! He's a new kid, sharp as a razor. He doesn't forgive…"

"And funny…"

"…And funny! Yeah! But you didn't like when I said that he's funny."

"He doesn't forgive, it seemed more appropriate than funny in our line of work!" Tom thought while thinking of the fine's incident. Then he said, "Never mind this funny bullshit, go fetch him, strip him out of the uniform and buy him some rags. Oh, bring him along." he smiled this time sarcastically. "I mean here in my office."

"He's not on duty today, sir!"

"Would that matter to you?"

"No sir!"

"And get the paparazzi out of this building."

"But lieutenant!"

"Go get this Gianni Russo! Go! I thought you understood the urgency!"

"Perhaps, sir, you should ask the…"

"…Chief?" I'll ask him later…oh, but you really don't understand the chaos we're in…"

"What's going on?" asked the other two detectives, Phil and Jim, as Dan stepped out.

"Stay the fuck out of his office unless he calls you!"

What a way to start a career for Lieutenant SanTommaso, an Italian born. The first thing he witnessed some twenty-five years ago, when he had set foot on the U.S. soil, just one month short of his twentieth birthday, was the distortion of his last name; St. Thomas or even worse St. Tom. And why had his parents given him Tommaso as a first name? What a ridiculous analogy with the last name of SanTommaso!

But on the office door the sign read: Lt. SANTOMMASO.

When Dan entered the police station with Gianni in his new attire, rags, the Uniforms, both men and women, looked with astonishment at the two of them.

"So what's going on Dan?" asked again the two other investigators as Dan and Gianni passed by.

"Beats me!" Dan hurriedly answered.

"May I?" Dan asked after the shy knock with his face between the door and its frame.

"Come in!"

Tom received them sitting behind his desk, titillating the palm of his hand on it. He took his hand off and raised his eyes above the frame of his reading glasses. He sternly looked at the young cop and quickly thought of the speeding ticket.

But Gianni, Tom noticed, had no intention to apologize for that incident.

"Twenty-five sir!"

"I don't remember asking you your age! He's reading my mind," Tom thought.

"Well! You were going to, no? Gianni just smiled.

"Can I have a cup of coffee?" he then asked.

"I'll get it..." Dan said.

"Not you! You!" Tom commanded to the other.

Gianni drifted out of the office. He knew the coffee was just an excuse to momentarily get rid of him. A cup was still fuming sitting on his desk.

He wanted to consult with Dan, for endorsement perhaps. What was Gianni, made out of it? Dan seemed to know him well.

"He's too young and too good looking. I think I met him once." Tom said wanting to smile. "Perhaps I wanted to forget him," he continued as if talking to himself but loud enough to reach Dan's ears.

"Forget him? Why forget him? For what?" Dan uttered confused. He always did get confused and easily disoriented when Tom made nonsense with words.

"I was only supposed to say that to myself but it came out loud enough to be heard. Forget it! Where were we?"

"He's sharp. He's very sharp." Dan continued in his endorsement for the young cop, however, still disapproving the fact that Tom didn't ask the chief's permission for the transaction he murmured, "It's not that I'm happy with clandestine decisions!"

Tom ignored it.

"He's sharp and funny," he said instead laughing contagiously taking Dan along. "Indeed, also very ambitious," he seriously sustained.

As Gianni put the coffee on the desk Tom thanked him and then asked, "What do you know about these murder cases?"

"All I read in the newspaper and from TV, of course."

"Do you think the three cases are related?"

"No sir. Not at this point in time, no."

"You have no doubt, that perhaps…"

"No sir! No doubt, unless things will develop differently."

"He's not just smart, he's a philosopher," Tom smiled. "He doesn't leave himself open. *Botta e contra botta!*" he thought in Italian. (Sharp reply to the point). "By the way do you speak Italian, since I'm assuming you are?"

"And Spanish and French…Oh, little bit of English, also."

Dan had stated that he was funny and guess what? He was!

All of a sudden, Tom analyzed himself against that kid. He has no doubts. He puts everything into prospective. Positive, so sure of himself…with audacity. He didn't give a damn about jeopardizing his career when he gave Tom a citation, which equaled about a quarter of his weekly salary.

One does not give a speeding fine to one's superior! But Gianni unattached to consequences showed integrity of character in the line of his job. Without a doubt, he did what he had to do. And that, Tom felt, was the gap between Gianni and him.

Tom lived and lives in doubts. Insecurities, worries and misconceptions, were all part of his life. He even doubted the unconditional love that his eternal fiancée Maria gave him, without asking for the reciprocal feeling in return. Thus, because of all the above, he had postponed their marriage three times. And it didn't help any that she had followed him to Florida. She genuinely loved him unconditionally. She let it be him!

The passage of time amid his adolescence and then youth towards maturity was tortuous and perilous without identity or direction. He wanted to be somebody but that somebody was nowhere to be found as of yet.

"I must find myself! I must find who I am and who I want to be. What role am I destined to assume in society?"

Thus during his few years of law school, out of boredom and because no vocation was yet at hand, he believed that a psychologist might ease his syndromes. He searched for one in the yellow pages and eventually found Doctor Snider.

"Two sitting hours for the price of one," read the terse and unique ad. And since, he was slowly and deeply influenced by the 'Americanization process', that ad appealed to him.

His first disappointment started at the first session.

Doctor Snider, had spirited eyes that blinked out of his tanned face like the blinking light in an obscure corridor's night lamp, which bulb announced the near end of life expectancy. Importunely Dr. Snider gave Tom no assurance at all. He wore his hair curly hanging over the neck. Tom didn't particularly like his aquiline nose. And the mouth that smiled two rabbit's front teeth. His appearance didn't encourage the patient-doctor relationship. Reflection, a splitting image of his profession, 'amazing', he thought. The pieces of the puzzle fit! And when the doctor pointed to him to sit on the chair opposite his, Tom murmured, "a chair? No couch? What happened to the luxury of laying on the so much celebrated pragmatic couch?"

Doctor Snider didn't answer the remark. Instead he just started his session with his first question, "So what seems to be the problem?" and a shower of saliva found its way to Tom's face. As he continued asking questions, his pupils rotated nervously upward, disappearing inside his upper lids while he compulsively pinched and tremulously adjusted his bowtie with his first two fingers. He tilted his neck to either side, according to the momentum of his arguments. Bewildered, Tom observed and diagnosed that the shrink was in an advanced stage of schizophrenia.

He decided to skip the free second sitting and with perseverance and commitment, he found his vocation. He pursued the law enforcement calling and never looked back on his past failures and indecisions.

The phone rang in his office.

"Okay! Okay!" Perhaps three more times he repeated, "okay," while Dan discreetly looked at Gianni without giving away the meaning of that look.

"Maria, tonight, I'll call you tonight." And click.

The phone rang again. A TV anchor's representative asked information about those cases. When he finished listening he just said, "You do that. Please inform me as soon as you find the killers and I promise I'll do something." And click.

Then silence fell upon the living space of the room.

"Sir, may I ask a personal question?" Gianni said.

"Anything as long as it's not about my girlfriend!"

"But of course not! You don't like coffee?"

While Dan stabbed an elbow on Gianni's ribs Tom just said, "Good observation! Get this kid out of here Dan! Gather information! Give him my cell number. I'm gone for the day. If the chief looks for me tell him it's my day off. Use my private number for emergency. The chief doesn't have it and you lost it if he asks you for it. This kid is now joining our squad. I'll talk to the chief about him on my way out." He said solely to appease

Dan whose scrupulosity about rules and regulations reached unknown limits to Tom. "And get those two out there to work. I've heard Jim Casa is a computer wizard. I want the names and the dossier of all ex-convicts in the county from the last two years till now."

"Lieutenant, it is a lot of work!"

"Do Jim and Phil have anything better to do?"

"No sir!

CHAPTER 3

▼

Lieutenant SanTommaso murmured within himself, "No bullets for the forensic, not a trace of fingerprints, not a hair, no blood other than the victims". Smooth job! Three different locations, approximately a few miles apart and a few hours apart.

An ex-priest strangled with evident signs of the brutal naked force of hands shielded by gloves.

A Rabbi stabbed in the chest twenty five times with what seemed to be an oyster knife.

A Minister left dead on the floor with a face disfigured with the forceful pounding of a baseball bat.

Nothing came from the coroner's butcher-table. The autopsy showed no fucking substantial evidence other than the cause of death already proven at the on scene investigation.

SanTommaso moved from Connecticut to Florida because of its balmy weather, its lakes. Because of that unreasonably calm and winding Intracoastal waterways that with its many inlets opens access to the Atlantic Ocean and, of course, its miles and miles of beautiful beaches, albeit not all as famed as South Beach!

Some people needed snowy mountains, farms, or extravagant places. He hated snow but needed water. The water cleansed his head, purified his brain, calmed him down and wiped his doubts away. Just to look at the sea running his eyes over the patches of blue and green ripples gave him solace.

He drove for half an hour without destination and smoked one cigarette after another. It was four o'clock and the sun was still warm. Hungry. He was hungry. He didn't have a bite to eat since the night before.

"What are you doing?" he asked as Maria picked the phone up.

"Nothing…I'm working on a project for my boss…"

"Nothing? Meanwhile you tell me that you're working on a project. Are you hungry?"

"No. Not really."

"No? Not really? What kind of an answer is that? Either you are or you are not!"

"Oh! Oh! You're upset…are those murder cases getting to you?"

"No! Piece of cake!" 'Bitch!' he wanted to say. Oh, how could he. She was so good to him? "I'm sorry," he murmured.

"For what?"

"For something I was thinking."

"If you come over I'll cook you something and we can talk about that something that you were thinking…"

"Nah! I don't want to take you away from your work…besides…"

"What?"

"I just wanted to tell you I love you."

"I love you too."

"I'll pick up a bite…I'll call you later. And click.

He drove northbound on A1A. Passed the town of Manalapan throwing one eye here and there at the waterfront mansions. Passed the Ritz Carlton driving along the condos that dominated on both sides of the road and separated the waterways from the ocean. He took a right turn into Lake Worth Municipal Casino.

He parked. Sat looking at the sea and then he stepped out. Hung his jacket on his big finger and swirled it over the shoulder. Then he walked the ramp that led to the pier. As he tried to open the gate a man warned him.

"Hey! Fifty cents to get in…" The voice came from a dark booth that resembled a chicken coop.

"I'm sorry," he just said and gave the man a dollar.

The man that wore pitch-dark sunglasses looked at him, smiled, returned the dollar and said, "I guess for you, lieutenant, it's on the house."

"Thanks! How the fuck does he know me?" he thought.

Slowly Tom crisscrossed the boardwalk and stopped at both edges to throw an eye below where the winding waves splashed around the posts that sustained the pier. Below the surface of the water, a bunch of barracudas were feasting on smaller fish. Tom looked at them and thought, "Criminal little sharks."

"How does he know me?" he asked himself again as the man in the booth that resembled a chicken coop flashed in his mind. The ringing of his cell distracted him. He looked at the Caller ID. He was Dan.

"Okay! What's up?"

"Sir! I'm thinking…"

"I'm happy for you! I can't!" He said and regretted the sarcasm. He knew Dan was a serious cop. He could turn out to be his right arm-man. "I'm sorry, what is it Dan?"

"That's okay sir, I can understand…"

"…Understand what?"

"Your sarcasm sir…"

"Okay, okay. Listen please! Although we know each other only a little while you and I…we related to these fucking murders. Okay I don't know what the fuck I'm saying. And please stop saying sir all the time…we're not in the military here or are we…? Are you hungry?"

"I could go for a bite!"

"Meet me at The Station House on Lantana Rd. I could go for a three-pound lobster. I'll call Steve he'll put us up in one of his smaller room. And we can talk."

"Can I put you on hold for a sec?"

"Sure!"

"I'm afraid it's not going to cut it. That was Jim Casa that called…"

"Okay! Shoot!"

"He has the ex-priest dossier…a mess! I think you better meet us at the station…"

"Okay! I'll be there! Is the chief in sight? Avoid him!" He then thought, "Skipping food again. At this rate I'll have anorexia nervosa within the month."

Jim Casa was already on the computer when Tom got there, preceding Dan. He raised his head and said, "I'm working on the Rabbi now, need ten minutes…"

Tom stood in back of Jim as he crisscrossed his hands frenetically while his nine fingers, one lost in an accident, banged on the keyboard with consumed passion.

"How does he see and read the material that spits on the screen." Tom thought.

"Sir, please? Don't stand in back of me…I…"

"Okay! Fine!" Then walking towards Dan he thought, "He plays the keyboard like Chopin played piano concertos." As he reached him, he softly asked, "Where is Gianni?"

"On his way here!" Dan whispered back. And the faint thread of his voice hardly reached Tom's ears.

"Nothing, nothing!" Jim shouted. "I need time, fresh wits, I need air." Thus he got up, shut down the computer and looked at the two of them in distress while an eerie silence fell upon the room.

Tom broke the silence, "Did you print the information on the ex-priest?"

"Yes sir!"

"Put it on my desk…let's all go for a bite…call Gianni and Phil and tell them to meet us at Dominique. You do know how to get there? Hypoluxo Rd west pass Jog on the plaza there!"

Of course! Dan knew!

"From Lobsters to pizzas, that's a switch," he thought. But then again with Tom one never knows. However, Dominique had a name to be the best pizza in town and the entries weren't that bad either.

It was already late evening. Tom thought of going to Maria but decided that a full night of sleep would be better. Start afresh the next day. Once in his apartment, he poured himself a glass of wine and lit a cigarette. He just sipped the wine, put the cigarette out and collapsed on the couch. And for two hours he fell into oblivion. He snapped out of it with his neck in a sea of sweat. He had dreamed of the young man he met at the Lake Worth pier; the one working at the booth that resembled a chicken coop. He was laughing at him with a toothless mouth; a grotesque face indeed. The opposite of what the pier attendant really looked like. He had a very pleasant and somehow handsome face. And perhaps a good set of eyes although the pitch-dark sunglasses totally obliterated them.

Tom shuffled to the bathroom and flushed his face with cold water. It was eleven. If Maria was still up, perhaps…why didn't he call her as he had promised? And why didn't she call him?

She had called. It showed on the Caller ID, at quarter after ten. He took the phone and pressed one.

"Did you call? What's going on?"

"Oh, nothing. I thought you'd come over," she said with her usual sensual tone of voice.

"Thought so too. I fell asleep on the couch."

"I…well, I feel lonely tonight…I feel like…you know I want to cuddle. You're not up to…perhaps…"

"Maria, honey! Are you going to make me feel guilty?"

"I'm sorry…"

"It was no use…one cannot fight with this woman," he annoyingly thought. Tonight a good healthy fight would be almost as good as a good night of sex. What a loser! Most men would give up their right arm for a relationship softer than puffy pillows. After years of tribulation and turmoil with other women, now that he had found a soul mate, he screws it all up by not being able to deliver.

Reluctantly, Tom went to see Maria.

She looked radiant. Every pore of her skin spoke of sexual desire. Her charcoal large eyes spoke clear of inner fire. The lit candles in the bedroom said it all. It was a signal, but more than a signal it was a ritual. Neither of them ever asked for sex. Anything could make it happen: a lit candle, an aria from the operas…

At five in the morning as he opened his eyes, Maria was still attached to his body. Softly, Tom slid off of her, kissed her on the forehead and went to shower. At six he was out of her house. He had slept a full four hours with no dreams, or nightmares. A beautiful morning indeed! He returned to the pier, unaware as if pulled by a mysterious inner desire. Perhaps the reason was hidden within himself and the joy to live a moment of tranquility. And the benefit to breath the salty air. Especially since again, just like the day before, the Atlantic Ocean slumbered, it seemed, in eternity. He wanted to just stroll around, relax and look here and there.

Oh the tender zephyr.

However, pulled by an unknown force, he quickly walked the ramp that led to the pier. As he reached the gate, he stood in front of the booth that resembled a chicken coop. The young man of the night before wasn't there. Tom hesitated a few seconds then said to the new attendant, "The fellow that worked here yesterday, is he off today?"

"Paul?" He doesn't work here."

"Last night he did!"

"Once in a blue moon, he chips in for me…"

"How can I get in touch with him?"

"You're not asking for much! Paul the invisible man! He's invisible. I don't even know where he's staying…although I know the few places he hangs around."

"Okay! Can you tell me?"

"No! But I'll tell him you're looking for him."

"It's important that I see him today…" he said landing a twenty-dollar bill on his lap.

"So, who are you?"

"Lieutenant SanTommaso!"

"Lieutenant who?"

"St. Thomas! Here give him my number. And with that he turned around and left.

It was late morning when he finally went back to work. Passing by Loren's desk, he wanted to stop for a quick chat with her. However, he declined the idea as he saw her flirting with a guy who leaned forward talking in her ear. Inside the office he found all his detectives there and a smoking cup of coffee sitting on his desk.

The cup of coffee brought in a smile. He nodded his head in approval and said, "Good morning and good luck!"

They all laughed.

Wouldn't it be beautiful if everybody in the whole world, in any office and working place, started the working days with a healthy laugh? Utopia!

"Lieutenant, Paul would like to see you for a few minutes…" Loren said on the intercom.

"Paul? Who's Paul? Ah! Paul! How the fuck does she know him?" He thought. Then he said, "I'll be right out. Guys, I'm sorry I need a good hour. Let's postpone the meeting and I'll meet you back here in an hour."

CHAPTER 4

▼

Paul's greeting was warm and pleasant, as if he were Tom's long time buddy. Tom didn't absorb the greetings well. His mind was too busy speculating about his connection with Loren. And why in hell this Paul, whose old pal at the gate called 'invisible man' comes so fast into his life? What was he doing whispering in Loren's ears?

They shook hands. Tom remained cool and austere. Paul turned his back to Tom, kissed Loren goodbye, and then quickly faced him again. With a touch of young arrogance he said: "I'm all yours!"

"I'll be back in an hour. Can I bring you something, soda perhaps?" Tom asked Loren.

"No, thank you sir," she timidly murmured. Instantly she felt her blood rushing to her face. The inquisitive but quick look in Tom's eyes spoke clearly to her that he, the chief investigator, wanted to know about their link. However, too quick of a look it was to cause her discomfort.

"I'll drive you! Behind the wheel, I'm the best money can buy." Paul said laughing.

Inside the car, Tom suddenly asked him, "What's the story with Loren?"

"No personal questions because you're not getting personal answers!"

"It's a deal! Why did you rush to see me? I can ask that, I hope. I don't recall giving your co-worker the impression of rush. A call would have been more than satisfactory." He lied concealing a smile.

"Easy, easy, lieutenant sir! That character you've met is not my co-worker and didn't give me your number yet. Granted I wanted to see you but mostly I wanted to see Loren…"

"Since I cannot ask you about Loren, what did you want to see me about?"

"I know of the three corpses you're investigating!"

"Do you work at the morgue?"

"I like you! Hum, good sense of humor. We're going to get along well…"

"I don't particularly like you! And I exhort you to make it fast."

"Exhort, big word, hum, for an Italian born, that's not bad."

"Paul, I don't have a lot of time available. I work for a living…by the way, prior to being an informant, what was your line of work?"

"You see, Lieutenant, I thought I made myself clear. No personal questions! Do you want information about the crimes? Just ask! Otherwise I'll drop you off…and as much as I'll regret it, goodbye to a beautiful future relationship."

Tom smiled within himself. He already liked him but he would be damned if he allowed Paul to see that.

"All ears! Shoot! Of course, you do have a price?"

Paul laughed. "For you? Not a penny! I like you!"

"As an Italian I only allow women to flirt with me!"

"Well okay! I'm independently wealthy. More than an investigator I'm a curious man. Since I don't need to work for a living…let's say it's one of my hobbies! At any rate, considering you're in haste, I'm going to start with the ex-priest's file—four brothers Irish born, two laymen, two priests, both excommunicated—The four brothers, with the last name of O'Connor, indiscriminately hate each other with passion. The reason escapes me and surely you don't to care about that. We're going to leave the two laymen alone. They reside in Ireland. As far as I know they haven't killed anyone yet and they haven't been killed either. They're still both alive and constantly at each other's throat. Our…Your concern and interest would be, I'm assuming, about the two ex-priests. The one on the loose, ex-Father George O'Connor; a womanizer. And the other, ex-Father Sean

O'Connor, alias the corpse; a pedophile. At this point allow me a comment: 'The two ex-priests embraced the Ministry not out of vocation but for the simple reason that the Catholic Church abounds with girls and boys.'

"*Pot-au-feu!* The prey is at hand!"

"Sounds like a fable...I'm supposed to believe you?"

"No! But back at the headquarters, compare my saying with Jim Casa's notes."

"You know Jim!"

"He's a crazy genius with that invention of the devil, almost as good as me!" He said pretentiously. "You're very lucky. Having him around will cut your work in half. Unfortunately, he's not stable and fails a lot for he goes beyond human capacity to prove a point. In fact his obstinacy to find things about me is going to kill him one of these days. However, I believe even without a file on me in this country he'll eventually find a piece or two of information..."

"But you already have pieces of information about him?"

"Of course! And of you...harmless bits!"

"Okay, finish the story..."

"A few years back Sean, the ex-priest, as I said before, a restless long-term pedophile beat the living hell out of his brother George. George, a restless long-term womanizer, took residence in the hospital for a month between life and death. Barely alive, but in one piece except for his dead right arm which was paralyzed since infancy, he initiated a sequence of deadly threats to the pedophile in the form of notes such as 'The anticipation of death is far worse than death itself'...and: 'Your time is up'!

"Too simplified!"

"Suit yourself!"

"Are you in possession of the notes?"

"No!"

"We're back to ground zero!"

"No, not yet! Whatever strength was missing in his right hand, George had it in his left."

"Why, did you read the X-ray?"

"You're funny…at any rate that's something to consider, although it may be of circumstantial nature. By the way, did you get the coroner's report?"

"Not yet!" He answered declining to give any information.

"Evidently you're surrounded by a bunch of lazy people…"

"Evidently you're also arrogant!"

If Jim's notes are comparable to Paul's information, Tom thought, then Paul could become a reliable future informant. However, so far his information constituted nothing but very fragile arguments. Can't bring those fragile arguments to the captain, the chief and consequently to the D.A. Tom had already been puzzled at the scene about the strange way Sean had been strangled. His neck, as he scrutinized the dead body, clearly showed one handgrip without any signs of any struggle. Tom wrote in his notebook; strange, only left hand-choke with no struggle.

Tom dismissed Paul postponing other information for later days and politely asked to be driven back to the station. Then he handed Paul a fifty-dollar bill.

"Lieutenant, you don't listen well. I don't work for a living. And evidently you have no interest to know about the other two crimes?"

"Wrong! I have no time left! I'll get back to you…besides I believe…well…it is in my character to work and finish one thing at a time. You've given me plenty of information for now. Thank you!"

That strange character, his arrogance, his alertness, his omnipotence, and the invisibility he pretended to possess, all bothered Tom. However, he had to admit that Paul had the qualities of a natural detective and that instantly made him likable in his eyes.

As he shuffled in the direction of his office passing Loren's desk, he quickly turned on his step and asked her, "What's Paul's last name?"

"Invisible, Mr. Paul Invisible!"

"Invisible? Mr. Paul Invisible?"

"Yes lieutenant!"

He thanked her and shook his head until he reached his chair. In a matter of minutes his assistants surrounded him. He apologized for leaving them and took the ex-priest file in his hand.

Loren came in with a smoking cup of coffee.

"Four brothers, Irish born, two laymen and two priests…matched, fucking matched as if Jim had given Paul the file to read," he murmured while he felt the eyes of all his men upon him.

"Sir," Dan shyly said.

"Yeah, Dan what is it?"

"The chief…the chief is looking all over for you. He was inquiring if you have a special number you could be reached…"

"You didn't give it to him?" alarmed asked Tom.

"No sir!"

"The chief…the captain? Did the captain ask you how we're doing with the investigation?"

"No sir! He just asked if you were okay! I told him you were!"

"When did you learn to lie?" he said smiling while the others burst into laughter.

"Lots of calls from the media." Dan continued after the laughter subsided.

"Take care of that. Talk positive. Tell them we'll come up with full details as soon as we have full details. However, if they insist on wanting to talk to me say that when more material is gathered, he'll be happy to speak to you. But at this particular point in time he'll decline to make unfounded comments just to please the media. Of course, you can use your own words. Phrase it to your liking. If, however, they ask if we have a suspect, tell them that when it comes to crimes the lieutenant believes everybody is a suspect until proven otherwise."

Then he stormed out of the office laughing.

Sitting across the chief's desk, Tom didn't follow a single word uttered to him. He was too busy speculating. Doubts of all sorts, doubts about everybody; his comrades and Paul. Yes, Paul? Who is he kidding? The killer's right arm has been paralyzed since infancy. What about a fake arm?

Vietnam veterans…they're plenty of men with only one arm among them in the county!

"Did you hear a word I've said so far," suddenly asked the chief.

"'Course I've heard you! What am I fucking deaf?"

He loved to play with words, "I haven't had food in ten hours. The fucking least you could do for me is to have one of those Uniforms schmucks out there bring me a fucking hot cup of coffee…"

The chief already hated that. Since Tom's first day at his job, he called his cops in uniform, Uniforms, but Uniforms schmucks…

"They are officers of the law! I would appreciate if from now on you'd refrain from making debasing remarks about them. Spare me! Have the fucking coffee that I was told you never drink, in your own office."

"It's mind over matter. Don't you read psychology?" he said ignoring the first part of the chief's reproach.

"Fuck psychology! We're running out of time…"

"We're not running out of time! It's the time that's running out…" Tom charmingly responded.

"Are you hungry?" The chief suddenly asked him. It was well known to all he was quick and good to change subjects for his convenience. He'd heard that when it came to good food, Tom knew it all.

"Of course, I'm hungry. I just got done telling you that my last meal is ten hours old. But right now it's absurd to think about food with all the *cazzi in culo* we're into." Tom said, not being too inclined to spend any length of time that necessity allowed in the chief's company.

"Dismissed!" The chief, irate, commanded. "We'll talk when your disposition is better!"

Smiling under his nose Tom left the room chopping at the eyebrows as in a military salute with the fingers of his left hand to remind himself that a left-handed man choked the ex-priest. He was still smiling when he entered his office, but a futile smile, for a sudden dizziness overcame him and an unexpected sweat ran over his shoulder. It was a prelude that he knew very well; the prelude to a nasty cold.

"I'll be damned," he thought, "if I'm not coming down with a nasty cold."

Only Maria was capable of alleviating the misery of coughing and of a stuffed or running nose. She was like his mother, full of tender and loving care when he was under the weather. Besides what a great lover Maria was.

He blamed the tourists, the northerners he called them, especially the snowbirds. In Connecticut he blamed the unstable New England weather. And in Sicily, when he was a young boy, he blamed the Asian just because he had caught *l'asiatica,* (the epidemic Asiatic flu). And he also blamed everybody for his discomforts. All sorts of daily miseries were always caused by new elements. There was always someone or something that caused all these things for him.

CHAPTER 5

▼

Fulfilled, Maria relaxed on the bed with a glow that made her face more beautiful. She was spellbound. Her half closed eyelids shadowed the large charcoal eyes. Then, she opened her lips to a radiant smile and from time to time, still in a haze, she looked at the snoring lover, softly touching his forehead for signs of fever.

"Amazing!" she thought on her way to the kitchen. How was it possible that with high fever, cough and stuffed nose during the past night, he'd made love to her with such a passion? And although still mesmerized, just thinking of it jumped her temperature to new heights like the sudden rise of mercury.

"He should come up with nasty colds more often," she murmured.

It was late in the morning when Tom woke up. He mumbled some scolding words at Maria for not waking him up earlier. She had his espresso ready, the only coffee he drank, and the shower on.

He gulped his coffee and jumped in the shower.

"Maria," he shouted from under the hot and splashing water. "Mari-aaaa! Bring me a towel...where the fuck are you?"

Maria pushed open the bathroom door, she glided back the shower curtain and with a towel in her hand, stark naked breathed, "Is this what you're looking for?"

"Yeah sort of...before...Maria, do you...I mean, perhaps you're too tired..." he murmured some aroused nonsense."

Maria quickly joined him with a bar of soap in her hand. Oh my god-oh-god-sainthomas-god-sainthomas-my-go-o-o-d-he-l-p...

CHAPTER 6

▼

At the office, Lieutenant St. Thomas instantly faced reality with such a force that his stomach churned uncontrollably. In a flash, gone were the idyllic moments spent in the company of his lover; the tender touches, the warmth of her lips, the sweaty ardor that fused their bodies into one, her final screaming, "oh god oh god…sainthomas…"

In the few mere seconds of orgasm she'd mentioned God more times than a priest preaching the gospel during Mass. And one never knows if Sainthomas was the apostle she was imploring or Tom himself?

All thoughts had instantly disappeared as Tom sat on his chair. The forensic reports on his desk piled up in loads with no proof at all. They were as lengthy as they were futile.

Three different locations, three different styles, three religious men of three different orders murdered, without signs of evidence or connection. Yet it seemed there was a basic connection among the three assassinations; at least judging by first sight. Yet Gianni Russo, the youngest and the least experienced detective, clearly and strongly had said without a trace of any doubt, "No connection sir!" And even Dan and Jim and Phil and even Paul, although they didn't quite openly state it, inferred no connection! At any rate, connection or not, the cases had to be investigated one at a time and Tom was doing just that. A lot of times when misconceptions of all sorts arose, he was forced to make the final decision. He had followed his gut feeling and had successfully achieved the end result.

Jim and Phil were assigned to pick up George O'Connor for interrogation.

Loren was assigned to get in touch with Paul and arrange a meeting with him sometime that same day. Even though he acknowledged that all her paperwork piled on her desk was plenty of assignment.

Dan's assignment had to do with visiting the other two victims' relatives and gathering information. As much as humanly possible, search, speculate and verifying behavior. Find their likes and dislikes, hobbies, cultural statuses, and their level of intelligence.

"Have I been clear?" Tom asked Dan, minutes later.

Dan wasn't too sure how clear Tom had been, but under the circumstances, he thought it a miracle that he had grasped most of his orders.

Nine Vietnam vets in the entire State of Florida had an amputated right arm or just an amputated right hand. Why, in the name of God, couldn't a few of them lose the left arm or the left hand? By elimination, the cycle of investigation would have shrunk.

Paul's cheerfulness put Tom on edge at the same moment he met him. A wealthy fuck! Perhaps uneducated, although his demeanor and his unusual but perfect diction of the English language surely showed the contrary. Perhaps it was jealousy! Damn right jealousy! Tom was born poor. He hated preppy spoiled kids of rich fucks. But Paul was not preppy. And he didn't seem spoiled either. Perhaps it was the mysterious lifestyle, the security that makes the rich man secure? Of course Paul's youthfulness bothered him the most.

Yet the perennial happiness, the brazen disposition that Paul displayed so naturally without makeup, appealed to him.

He claimed to be independently wealthy. Money was the evil! Yes money! But money and misery get along so well! But misery without money brings even more misery. That train of thought left him instantly when Paul entered his office smiling with extended hand to shake Tom's.

"Lieutenant, may I call you Tom? It makes it easy to communicate."

"Call me any fucking name you want. I don't feel like a lieutenant or chief investigator. I don't feel like anything. I don't even know why I had

Loren arrange a meeting. And as for you…well, do you really think sitting on the fucking computer makes you a detective?"

"I do have information off the computer. Give me a minute of your time and I'll pass it on to you." Paul said with a look of compassion on his face that irritated Tom.

"Make it quick!"

"Sean O'Connor had a fixation with electrical wires."

"I'm listening…" he sighed without conviction.

"In short he knew about electricity more than electrical engineers…"

"What has that to do with my investigation? Why would that interest me? I really don't think you have any new material. You're trying your best without having any best to offer."

"You know at the rate you're going you'll end up in a mental institution! The least you could do is to listen. Let me finish! George also has a fixation with electricity; the only thing in common between the two brothers. The few times, very few, that peace reigned within them, they worked together on crazy mechanical and electrical gadgets; toys of any kind."

Tom dismissed Paul with haste. "However," he said with a tinge of sarcasm, "I'll consider your story, but for the time being I must to go. I would give you more time, however my work is so overwhelming that it limits me to enjoy more of the social time than perhaps I'm allowed. Goodbye Paul, I'll talk to you soon!" Then he walked him to the door.

Maria was preparing snapper for supper, one of his favored meals. He was looking forward to eat, drink his bottle of wine and just be at ease. Thinking about the leisure time in the company of his lover instantly cleared his face from the past tenseness. He calmly drove to the Yacht Club in the town of Hypoluxo where Maria had her residence, humming the lyrics of an Italian song. He stopped at the gate and flagged the card wedged between his two fingers, hesitating to insert it in the box. Instead he backed up to US1, made a hasty left skidding swing and drove to Sean O'Connor's house. As he was speeding, thoughts of his mother flashed back. A young adult then, she had scolded him for he didn't believe much of anything—*San Tommaso vedere e toccare e poi credere*—a passage of the New Testament.—St. Thomas: to see and touch is to believe!

He entered the house slowly and circumspectly through the lower window he'd purposely left unlocked when leaving the crime scene. Although legal access to the crime scenes was within the rights of jurisdiction, he had chosen since the beginning of his career to never lock windows. The reasons escaped everybody, including himself.

Once inside he stood still, not in fear but apprehensively tense. Deaths, ghosts or anything creepy might just about jump off the walls and grab him by the shoulder. After a deep breath, he quickly ran his eyes everywhere. Nothing unusual.

"Nothing!" he said blaspheming. "No wires other than the house's electrical system and no suspicious buttons!" If what Paul said was correct the house should look like an electrical repair shop. Frenetically, more to prove Paul wrong than appease himself, he ransacked and tossed around every piece of furniture ripping the better part of it all. When in that state of mind, Tom was capable of being a little too daring; messing up with the crime scene could get him in trouble.

No! No signs at all, not even one simple electrical tool.

Doesn't, an electrical freak, worker, or engineer need tools? How does one cut, twist, solder or bond the whole motherfucker ordeal?

Vomit's sensations for lack of food and for that damned chain-smoking routine prickled his gums as if he had suddenly contracted trench mouth. Under the kitchen faucet he scooped the palm of his hand and filled it with water. He sucked it out, gurgled and spit it out. He ran his eye long range at the mess he had created and then exited from the same low window. He readjusted the police yellow tape that the wind had ripped out and drifted to the front door. He stood there awhile and then dialed Maria's number to tell her he was going to be late.

The door sprung open hissing so loudly that he simultaneously ducked down and blocked his ear with the palm of his hand to avoid severe damages to his eardrum.

"What the fuck!" he swore. He thought he had been electrocuted. From his cell the operator repeated over and over, "I'm sorry your call did not go through as dialed, you must hang up and try your call again."

He sat on the stairs in deep silence looking all around, and then he murmured, "I must have dialed the wrong number when the door sprung right open. I hit a code. Strange! I must dialed the wrong number, or missed one all together. It's a code," he uttered.

"Open Sesame!" he laughed. "It's a piece of luck. A flower blossomed in my ass."

But what number? Which one? Quickly seized by frenzy he dialed again and Maria picked up.

"Shit!" he swore.

"Why?" Maria answered. "I'm not supposed to pick up...?"

"Of course! Honey listen I'm going to hang up. I'll call as soon as I'm done. Something happened. I'll tell you later."

"Are you okay?"

"Don't call me back on my cell." And click!

Analyzing facts, he first thought to call a Bell South's technician to find the number, then smiling, he murmured, "Bell South my ass...Jim! Jim! Jim knows more about things like that than any Bell South's technicians." He dialed the station, Phil answered.

"Jim, get me Jim on the phone."

"He's momentarily out."

"Find him! And all of you come to Sean's house!"

Ten minutes later he heard the sirens.

Yeah! Perhaps he's tough with his guys. He gives them little credit. He annoys them with his fucking sarcasm. But that small group of detectives was the best he ever had. Each one of them was different in character and shape but united with the same spirit of resolve.

Tom explained to Jim what had happened, ignoring the others who waited in silence and disbelief.

"And you want me to find that number?" Jim asked.

"Yes! Of course!"

"You're kidding lieutenant! Please tell me that you're kidding!"

"No!" Tom said, handing him the cell.

However frustrated, Jim responded by taking the cell off Tom's hand. He cradled it in the palm of his hand then murmured, "Okay I'm ready!"

"Wait!" Tom said and went to shut the door.

As he had done with his computer when given his first assignment, he ran his nine fingers on the numbers pad with the same dexterity that Chopin had when he ran his ten fingers over the piano.

Tom looked at his watch every few minutes. He paced the floor back and forth while gazing at Jim's shoulder, spying on the cell.

"Lieutenant! If you don't stop looking over my shoulders we're not going anywhere here! Goddamn!" he dared to say.

"Okay, okay…I'm sorry!" he mumbled and moved yards away.

Thirty minutes had passed by and the damned door didn't move.

"I need a cup of coffee," he wanted to say and for the first time since being on the job he didn't dare to ask. Dan and Phil looked at each other and felt the vibes.

"Without the fucking coffee that he never drinks he is climbing walls." They murmured at the same time. And that almost prickled them to laugh, but smartly and quickly chocked it. Instead Phil's eyes focused the desire to Dan that perhaps one of them could run to the nearest coffee shop. Anticipating, however, that the rustle of drifting would distract Jim Casa and seize him into a frenzy of the devil, Dan remained immobilized throwing a disapproving stare at Phil. Besides, they were sure that the problem would soon be solved and then Tom could have his coffee that he won't drink. That crazy kid running his nine fingers that worked like a hundred on that gadget will soon succeed and the door will spring open…

…And the door sprung open with a jarring to set teeth on edge.

Openmouthed, they just stood there looking at Jim. He didn't move, but signs of stress could be read in his eyes and on his forehead that dripped bubbles of sweat. He looked at the cell, then swept with the back of his hand the bubbles of sweat and chucked the cell against the wall.

"Fucking little asshole," he shouted.

The phone's broken bits rebounded and splashed around.

"My phone? How am I going to piece it together? And the ultimate number that made the code…?"

"I'll buy you a new one! And not just the ultimate number but all the numbers are up here!" he said nervously pointing his finger at his head.

The roar of laughter was inevitable!

After the euphoria wore off, Jim just said with a thread of voice, "I'm sorry lieutenant."

"Piece of cake!" Tom murmured with a concealed smile.

The other two didn't know if they should keep laughing or shout hurray and take Jim on their shoulder like fans do with sport's idols. They loved that kid! He was so young and fragile. He didn't belong with the tough guys. But give him a computer, a keyboard, a cell or anything with numbers and letters of the alphabet and his fragility turned into a brutal and powerful force.

Dan, as usual in conformity with rules and orders, didn't want to move his first gigantic step inside the house.

"Perhaps we should make contact with the scientific squad…perhaps call in the coroner…"

"Perhaps we should just keep the whole fucking ordeal to ourselves for now!" Tom answered with a specific mean voice while nodding his head.

Meanwhile Gianni Russo, who evidently couldn't reach Tom because his broken down cell rested miserably in peaces on the floor, called Dan and asked to pass him.

"Yeah Gianni what's up?"

"The sheriff from the Sheriff's Bureau of Crime Investigation wants you to call him."

"Sure! Like all the other agencies that agency also wants a piece of my ass! Dan, call the sheriff I'll talk to him now. Oh, use your cell! Mine is out of whack forever!" he said mildly this time, concealing a smile.

"What's going on Lieutenant Tommasso…?"

"…SanTommaso, Sheriff…" Tom corrected him a bit on edge. Perhaps thinking the sheriff purposely cited his name incorrectly.

"Yeah! What's going on?" the sheriff asked again.

"What's going on what?"

"With the investigation! Of course!"

"Beats me sheriff!"

"Lieutenant, my boy! Are we going to play games? I've heard you're a tough cookie…"

"…Tough cookie? On the contrary, sheriff, I'm a soft cookie. But the kind that explodes on the mouth that takes a nasty bite off of it.

"Don't need to get off like that…"

"Sheriff what is it? What can I do for you? I'm trying to work here. Get to the point…"

"Okay, okay lieutenant. I've called you to make you aware that if you're in need of some help you can count on me. Our investigation bureau is equipped with the latest forensic lab…with newest technology, if I may say so…"

"Sheriff! We're not at that point. We'll consider it though. I haven't eaten since yesterday! Can I detail things for you tomorrow? Tomorrow, sheriff, tomorrow…have a good night sir!" And click!

"Fucking asshole!" the sheriff murmured but his phone dial tone made him aware the communication was off.

Tom had told Gianni to bring over a wire detector. The two brothers were definitely electrical freaks, just as Paul had deduced. The hibernated wires were there; codes, buttons, and other electrical elements…Perhaps outside the house underground…weren't they electrical geniuses? They searched every corner of every room. The detector didn't sound different than the usual, and then suddenly it buzzed. Their ears stood up in alert. They looked at each other and quickly ripped off parts of the wall with their hands like trained pigs that tilt the ground with their paws in a hunting frenzy for truffles. A complex circuit of twisted taped wires, all crisscrossed and serpentine, led to other boxes all with red and black buttons. The New York subway system was less complicated.

In amazement the detectives looked at each other, then turning to Tom they asked in unison, "How did you get to know about it?"

"Tip-off, imagination and luck! Also the forensic report showed no fingerprints. And the relentless squeeze on the neck of the fucking *finocchio* brought me to believe that an electrical prosthetic right hand was used for the job, which will bring this investigation to ground zero. Can't prosecute an electrical prosthetic arm, even if it is found, unless we find the person that put the finger on the button of the operational system. However we've been here three hours and there's no sign of it."

Just before leaving the house and when all that fails had failed, they found an exposed bit of wire that led them to the rest of the system. By pressing on that wire a hermetic encased large board unsealed from the wall. It glided and rested in mid-air. The top displayed a miniature train station equipped with trains, waiting areas, bathrooms, a ticket office, and some passengers. With a simple touch of the remote control encased under the table, the big toy synchronized its movements as in a real station. They found many other things but none that resembled a fake hand or arm.

Disappointed, tired, sweaty, with a look on their faces that smelled anger and frustration, Tom ordered them to wrap it up.

"Tomorrow! No! Tomorrow I'm summoned to meet the chief. We will comeback the next day. By then my mind will be clear and fresh from the chief's nonsense. Good night!"

"Good night Lieutenant!" they all answered.

CHAPTER 7

▼

It was one in the morning when he stepped inside his apartment. The refrigerator was empty. He drank a full glass of wine that nauseated him a few minutes later. Then he hit the bed. He tossed in the bed like when he was sixteen and fell in love for the first time. He sweated a pail of sweat and then dozed. Suddenly shaken by a nightmare he couldn't recall, he sat up and put the light on. He went for one more glass of wine forgetful that the first one had nauseated him.

He slumbered again.

When he woke up at five, he had barely slept two hours. He took a cold shower. Alert and fully awake, he went straight to his office to go over some papers and mentally prepare himself before stepping into the chief's office.

Meanwhile Phil had discovered that Rabbi Greenwald had a million dollar insurance policy. His wife, Andrea, was anxious to cash in, since she was the beneficiary, which made her a prime suspect.

Dan, charged with renewed vigor, plunged headlong into the investigation of Rev. Sid Morgan. With Jim's report in hand he found out that, among other things, the Reverend was a filth, and filthy rich sixty year old bachelor. He had never been married but was never without a female companion, who was never older than twenty something. The last had been with him the longest. Moira, besides being of rare beauty, had also a rare appetite for luxury. In her closet, among designer dresses and outfits of all sorts, Dan had found three hundred pairs of shoes; all imported from Italy.

Dan painstakingly took Moira in as a prime suspect to interrogate her.

Gianni Russo set in with the unusual task of going over the investigations that both Dan and Phil had already been empowered with.

Of course, nobody could take Jim away from his computer. And it was just as well. Tom and all of them didn't even know if Jim could fire a gun. Besides, they had become so protective of him that if one of these days he came up with a common cold, they would rush him to the Emergency Room.

Tom, doubt or no doubt, was getting confident about the investigations. Later on, however the connections, as it were discoursed upon, were full of gaps and loose ends and they fell through. Again he felt left in a maze of suppositions, with only flimsy evidence and no light at the end of the tunnel.

At the chief's office, Tom stood in silence with his reeking cup of coffee in one hand and a cigarette in the other. He took a long drag on the cigarette and exhaled the smoke away from his superior. However, the puffs went straight towards the chief's face.

"I can understand," said the chief looking with pity at Tom's eyes while turning his face sideways to avoid the smoke that insisted on reaching his nostrils, "that without that fucking coffee and that fucking cigarette, which smug is following me, your performance might lose its momentum. But, indeed, I must say that playing with those two grownup toys is not helping our common cause. And you're aware, of course, that smoking is prohibited inside buildings all over the fucking state of Florida"

"Chief," Tom answered, "if you've called me to insult me, please, spare me! And let me remind you that although, I am a responsible officer of the law, I am also a citizen of this splendid country of ours and as a citizen I have the sacrosanct right to vote for whom or what I like…and for your information I voted against smoke prohibition. Our country has a history of prohibitions of which I'm not pleased at all. As far as the investigations, it takes time and resolve. I…we, are in synch. Give me permission to carry on."

Three Italians and two Irish men, the chief was thinking and he nodded his head. The damn combination could drive his agency and others including FBI's, into *delirium tremens.*

"By the way, Tom…how did I look?" he lightheartedly asked with an unexpected poised smile.

"How did you look where?"

"On CNN? Don't you watch the news? How did I look?"

"No! I didn't see you! No time to watch TV!"

"By the way Tom, you and I wear the same size, perhaps next time I'll be summoned to appear again…we must satisfy the media. You know! We must keep on good terms with the media, as you should know! At any rate, perhaps I could borrow one of your finer suits?"

"One of my finer suits? Damn right they are fine! But do you know what you're asking me? Worth Ave, I buy them in the shops on Worth Ave. You figure the price, you're good with numbers…granted," he thought but never said it, "Ill buy them at summer clearance, 75% off."

"Get the fuck out of here! And don't step foot in this office unless you bring in cuffed assassins. Dismissed. Permission to carry on, granted…"

On the way to his office he met the captain in the corridor and barely saluted him.

"Tom? What is it? You look awful!"

"Do me a favor captain…"

"…Captain? What's the formality?" he smiled.

"Bob!" Tom said calmly, "do me a favor, and get the chief off my fucking back. He's driving me up a wall!"

"I'll get him off. I promise," said the captain putting his arm around Tom's neck. Then the two of them burst into laughter when Tom told him the chief asked his opinion on how he looked on TV.

"Tell me you're kidding me."

"He also asked me if he could borrow my suits for the following occasions!"

"Tell me you're fucking kidding me?" he kept on saying as he, laughing, left Tom.

His men were in the office waiting. They expected to see him frustrated. It was a fact, the chief's demands and the nuisance that went with it, frustrated Tom. But to their great surprise he walked in cheerfully and greeted them cordially.

"If one of you will get me a cup of coffee I'll tell you what the chief wanted to know," Tom said with a conspiratorial smile within himself.

"Stay put!" Dan said to Jim who offered to go get it, "I know how to make it just the way he likes it."

The roar of laughter picked up a new momentum minutes later when Tom told them the very reason the chief summoned him. "Imagine, he wanted to know how he looked on TV and if he could borrow one of my suits." Then he paused a second, and he looked at Gianni. Sensing a sudden change of mood in the young detective he asked, "What's on your mind Gianni?"

"Well...I...lieutenant! I know! I had foolishly admitted no connection among the three cases, but going over and over what Phil and Dan came up about the Rabbi and the Minister, it seems..."

"...It seems there's a connection!" Tom stated.

"Yeah...it seems. But as far as the ex-priest I have not yet been able to tie the knot."

"What do you think about that?" Tom asked Jim.

"Jim smells it also," continued Gianni cutting in for his partner whose mind perhaps was entangled by new mathematical dilemmas.

"The common life style! All three as rich as the pope yet away from their religion living a mischievous life. We have here a dead Rabbi whose gorgeous wife, according to the most recent information, made him 'cornuto' cuckold not once but nine times over. Reverend Morgan was living in sin with a twenty something year old beauty that could make the Tower of Pisa finally get its former erected position...of her we do not know as of yet, of any clandestine affairs. And as far as the ex-priest, unfortunately we have, as of now, no information prior to his assassination of a co-habitant, male or female. Although we know of his preferences, we know nothing about his sex life. His brother who at this very moment, is under investigation as a prime suspect, says he couldn't get it up for shit, not with boys and surely not with girls."

"My suggestion to all of you is to keep working on the investigation with an open mind, meaning: thoroughly follow through with your prime suspects. Remember! Everybody is guilty until proven innocent. God speed I'll see you tomorrow!"

He sat at his desk after everybody left, looking at his coffee. Tempted to get a sip out of it, he took the cup in his hand, cradled it a few times and replaced it on the desk. Then he peeped outside the door at Loren.

"Loren, can I…?"

"Yes sir!" she answered with a jerk.

"Can I see you a moment?"

It was the first time he had not used the intercom when he needed her. She felt this was more like a personal call and as she walked in she suddenly blushed. As she felt the heat rushing to her cheeks, she quickly and unaware placed the cup of coffee on the desk and hid her face between her palms. Then she forced a smile.

"Please," he said gently, aware of her discomfort. "Please have a seat," he encouraged her, genuinely smiling back at her. Then as she hesitated to sit, he, with a slight and gentle wave of his hand, indicated the chair in front of him. Once she sat, he somehow clumsily, said, "I have to ask you a few personal questions…if you feel uncomfortable and intimidated and don't want to answer, just say so! Or just answer what you can."

"Okay!" she just mumbled.

"Can you tell me anything at all about Paul?"

As she hesitated, Tom continued, "Before you answer me, I want you to know that I would not put you in any jeopardy no matter what your answer is. And I'm not going to judge you either…I'm not here to judge anybody. Is Paul your, you know…boyfriend?"

"Yeah! Sort of!" She mumbled.

"Sort of?"

"We go out a lot, but no commitment!"

"Doesn't it bother you that little is known about him? He's living a mysterious life in a world of connections and friendship? Nobody can find him and yet he is around like a real invisible man?"

"In the beginning it did, but he's such a gentleman...he treats me kindly...I just don't ask. He doesn't like to be asked personal questions!"

"Do you love him?"

She ignored the question and he, although in wonder, ignored her silence.

"Invisible or not you must know where he's staying, an apartment a house?"

"Perhaps he's playing games because of his last name. I haven't known him long enough to answer that! But can I ask you a question?"

"Of course!"

"Is he a suspect or something?"

"No! Absolutely not! I like him, I like him very much but as a man of law and order and as a detective, his character throws me off. Inquisitively speaking that should also bother you! After all you're an officer of the law also! How do you get in touch with him? His phone?"

"The cell! Okay! Let me make it easy. He stays at the Breakers a lot, and the Ritz Carlton, a month at a time...sometimes also at the Four Seasons! Depends on the mood he's in."

"And you stay over...some time..."

"...Some time?"

"You're living a deluxe life..." he chuckled. "On your...on our salary...we couldn't even afford to sit on one of the sofas in their lobby!"

"He's got money, lots of money. He covers me with expensive gifts and extravagant dinners. I like it..." she shyly smiled.

"I too would like it!" His wise smile turned her chuckle into a quick but short laugh. "And you never question him where the money comes from?" he said after her giggles wore off.

"Once or twice! But he never answers back...he's not in trouble is he lieutenant?" She shyly questioned him again.

"No! Be sure of that! Just curiosity...our job made me curious. I can't stand it when I don't know things about people." he said with a hard laugh now taking her along. "I'm sorry I took you away from your work. One of these days when I get the chief in a cheerful mood, which I find hard to imagine, I'll recommend you for a new and better position!"

"I like my position! I like working for you…" was her shy but straight-forward answer.

"Okay then! I'll recommend you for an increase in salary!" he said seriously.

When Loren was gone, he sat for a long time with his hands behind his neck and stared at the ceiling. His eyes blinked at the ringing of the phone. He suddenly returned to earth. It was Maria's call. The blinking light gave her away. It was the number she dialed before his cell if he didn't pick up.

"Yeah what's up?"

"Are you aware I haven't seen you in a week and last time you called, it was three days ago?"

"Is it that long ago, imagine how time goes by?" he just said. Then he burst into laughter, however quickly covering the mouthpiece, for one of his best friend's favorite joke came to mind.

Two friends: one the landlord, the other his tenant.
Since the tenant was a few months late on the rent, the landlord, tired of waiting, paid his friend a visit. 'Compare' the landlord said:—Do you realize you're three months late on the rent?
—Sincerely? That long? Dear God how time flies!

That night Tom went to Maria's. She had prepared a marvelous dinner and the wine wasn't bad either, but Tom was distant and taciturn. He only broke his silence to answer her questions, and that was just to approve or disapprove them. He just murmured: yes, no, of course!

Maria looked radiant. The CD played his favorite music. He undressed and quietly went to bed.

Maria took a quick shower, put on a fancy negligee, and lay next to him.

Tom was snoring like a pauper.

C H A P T E R   8

▼

Tom heard much more than he could stand about Moira's beauty, Rev. Morgan's concubine.—One can get into a trance by just looking at her. What an ass, and the fucking tits...Et cetera-

He ignored their nonsense for a while, however temptation got the best of him.

"Both of you!" he shouted to Dan and Gianni, "you're coming up with nothing with that broad! You can't pay attention to what she says if the ass and the tits get in your way. That is not the investigation's way! Call her!" he commanded ignoring the two cops' sarcastic smiles. "Make me a date...arrange me a meeting. I want to check her out. I mean interrogate her."

The meeting was scheduled at her residence at six pm.

He stood in hesitation at her door. Moira spying through the keyhole saw him procrastinating. Thus she suddenly opened the door fully as Tom put his knuckles ready to knock. He stumbled half way inside almost colliding with her.

"Take it easy, Lieutenant SanTommaso you almost knocked me out of my socks! Do you always move that fast?"

"Not really Miss. Moira...you caused my unbalance when you decided not to wait for me to knock!" he said quickly running his eyes over that splendid creature. "At any rate, good evening, Miss. Moira. Could you invite me to come in?"

"Only if you drop the Miss!" she said now waving her index finger in his eyes with an arrogance that might or might not reflect her personality. The brazen frankness of that moment did not convince Tom at all, of legitimacy, but the aura of sensuality and splendor that seemed innate in her, that surrounded her, did. That was real. That confused him, yet inebriated him.

"Is it really anybody's business who the fuck she kills? One is bound to die in her bosom anyhow!" he mumbled within himself while he followed her to the living room. Totally taken by her curvaceous body's movements that could not be contained by her robe, he stumbled along. And as if that weren't enough to perturb him, Moira's next move blew his mind. She offered him to sit on the easy chair. Then, purposely choosing the chair that faced his, she slowly, with premeditated coquetry, sat crossing her legs letting one flap of her robe drop open exposing her radiant thighs. Tom, instantly as if taken by an uncontrollable force, sinuously stretched his neck with his eyes popping out of the orbits as if attached to the end of two springs, like the character of a scary movie. They insinuatingly stared with stupor at the darkness of her groins.

"Beautiful legs? Are they not?"

"Sure! Definitely!" he said shaken. "But I'm not here to admire your legs…I came to talk to you about your…your…Reverend Morgan."

"Tom! May I call you Tom?"

"Sure anything, I mean, of course!"

"There isn't much to talk about…didn't detective Macday tell you of my alibi?" she answered without arrogance while a tinge of mellowness spoke clearly that the only arrogance she was endowed with was the arrogance of her beauty. Deep down he just knew she was a soft and gentle woman.

"Of course! But I'm in charge! I'm here to close the case," he said thinking that perhaps if he doesn't shorten the visit he might just about lose the case. "I need you to answer a few innocent questions…"

"…Innocent questions? There's nothing innocent about you Tom!" she wittily said.

"Perhaps…you're right about that," he answered between bursts of laughter. "However," he continued seriously, "I have to write a report, and God knows how accurate one must be! You do understand that! I hope?"

"It was awful to look at Sid's disfigured face. What a horrible homicide that was. Granted, I was not in love with him, I perhaps used him, although I also cared for him. To die a terrible death like that…" she said all that with so much humanity and humbleness while tears ran along her cheeks.

Tom was suddenly captivated. He completely ruled out that she could have been the maker of such an atrocious crime. However, the reality of it all was that he had many times witnessed women crying of innocence during interrogations who, however, were afterward proven guilty. Perhaps, he thought she was a partner behind the curtain, a silent partner. In effect, although he still didn't believe it possible, she could have been an accomplice. The sobbing that broke down her words, the sound of her voice, brazen and impertinent at times, mellow and sweet other times during the conversation, confused Tom. Following every word and every facial expression, he came to the conclusion, the one he wanted to believe, that the only thing guilty about her, was her beauty. Then his mother flashed in his head with the old saying of many years ago: St. Thomas, to see and touch to believe!

"You played Baseball?" he suddenly asked. "Up to the age of 16 with the boys and if I read it right the local newspaper of that time said, 'you played it better than them. In fact, top of the line,' it said you were."

He suddenly stopped talking, intent looking at her honey brown large eyes with eyelashes that curled up like feathers. He glanced at her thin yet sensual lips, quickly running his eyes over her body stopping at the curve that ended at her spine. Then he stopped his eyes at her endless beautiful legs. Her polished suntan gave him an instant urge of lust.

"What?" she exclaimed confused for she also felt lust on its way

"Oh…well…nothing!" he mumbled feeling caught in the act. "Definitely!" he thought right after. "She's not just top of the line. She definitely stands at the top of the line!"

"Yes!" she admitted after that moment of alluring perdition. "I was better than the boys. I have all my bats except the one that was used! You do know that! Someone took it and used it, perhaps to incriminate me. I was told you are holding it as a murder weapon."

"Not me, the coroner! Our investigators just found it in a pond near the house. That's also given us trouble to clear you and close your case for good. The coroner is working on it. He needs to see if some blood stains other than yours can be found…I mean recent stains, you know. Your old stains don't make you a suspect, however it's a cause to bring you again into a short and meaningless investigation. Perhaps, it's also possible that the bat we have is not the one used for the murder. In fact if you know different, I suggest you help me find the right one. It would make it easy to prove your innocence! The right bat will bring us closer to the batter."

"I was at my sister's! You know that…"

"But our prosecutors are nasty creatures and they can easily prove your sister is your accomplice or vise versa. There is a lot of money that disappeared in connection with the assassination that could have been the motive for the killing."

"Tom," she cried again like a little baby now. "You're telling me I'm in deep trouble…"

"Not if I can help it! But you have to level with me. Tell me all about the people that visited this house. Open up to me. Don't look at me as the head investigator. Look at me as your friend, someone who wants to help you! Talk to me about strange things. Things that made you wonder and that raised your suspicions. His friends, enemies, we all have some of them, all of us, Moira. Even if at that time it didn't mean anything to you. It is imperative that I know every detail. Every little bits, an improper sneeze…if I may say so! All, please, tell me all!"

"Why do I like you when I think you're here to screw me up?" she said sighing.

It took him time to recuperate from the equivocal double meaning of the word. He wanted so badly to make a sexual innuendo based on it. Instead he just said, "You might not believe it but I, sometimes, am likable…"

"I believe it!" she said smiling and sobbing at the same time, which gave Tom goose pimples. "I…I'm so afraid I can't sleep at night. What if the same guy would do me for whatever reason he did Sid?"

"If that bothers you that much I can give you round the clock protection!"

The phone rang and she talked to the person on the other line quietly for a few minutes. Then she hung up.

"Who's that?" he just asked.

"A friend of Sid. I'm assuming…"

"…Assuming, you're assuming he's a friend of Sid. What's his name? I've just fucking told you if I must help you, I must know it all," he shouted at her. And with anger he suddenly stood up and quickly drifted towards the exit. "Evidently you do not need my help!" he shouted again turning as he neared the door.

"Wait, wait! God mercy!" she called running after him. "You're so fast you don't give me time to think."

"We don't have time if I must protect your ass, if I may say so…"

"Please Tom!" she pleaded putting her arm around his waist while placing her head softly against his shoulder like a little kitten looking for love, attention and protection.

"He calls himself Peter…"

"You're fucking still playing games with me…at the rate you're going, the can will be your new residence and the electric chair your salvation. Alibi or no alibi, I promise you!"

"Please Tom be gentle with me. You scared me so much my stomach is churning…I swear it to God I don't know this man and I have never met him. He called Sid a lot."

"And you still have the audacity…"

"Please," she implored him. "You must believe me! I'm telling the truth!" She cried loud now and while sobbing she continued, "He has a specific recognizable voice…a particular tone of voice, kind of a cadenza, one can pick it up amid a crowd."

"Clear that for me, I've lost you!"

"The few times I picked up the phone when he called for Sid…" She kept on sobbing. "I was always capable to know it was him because of his unique voice or whatever you want to call it."

Tom looked into her eyes and marveled so much wanting to hug her and comfort her. He wanted to wipe her tears with each one of his fingers and dry them one by one with care and sympathy as if he was not the head investigator. For God's sake there's no room for sympathy in his line of work. Rough, he has to appear. He has to keep his feelings separate.

"What did he want? Why did he call you?" he suddenly asked strongly.

"Nothing specific. He asked me if everything was fine with me and he'll get in touch. He scares me. He doesn't know me well enough. I don't know him at all. Why all of a sudden all this attention? He scares me!"

"If you level with me, if you're honest, I'll get you protection!"

"I swear I am. Tom, please believe me!

He did believe her. Strange he felt, but he believed her. He quickly dialed Dan to prove to her what he was capable of.

"Yeah," Dan answered. He was off duty but he'd be damned if he would piss him off. Lately he barked at everybody and everything. But Dan found in the other end of the line, a soft-spoken Tom, gentle in every way.

"Dan I'm sorry to bother you at this late hour. I need you to do me a favor first thing tomorrow morning. Get me four Uniforms out of the uniform to watchdog Moira round the clock. And Dan? Just between us. Please don't ask the chief for permission…"

"But Tom?"

"Please! If he happens to find out, the captain will get us off the hook! I'll talk to Bob tomorrow." And click!

It was time to go. From six to ten, four hours he had been with Moira and for what, besides feeling sorry, and empty inside.

As he bid goodnight, Moira murmured, "Now that I was getting used to your anger you're leaving."

Leaving? Who the hell wanted to leave? Not Tom! That's for sure. To leave was not a desire. It was a damned duty. Absolutely an obligation! Not to Maria, not to anyone else but to himself. Self-inflicted, self-imposed obligation it was, an obstinacy of disproportional strength of character. He owed it to himself, to the position that he held and to his integrity.

"May I give you a kiss good-night?" she shyly asked seeing that his decision to leave was irrevocable.

"It's not that I'm off duty," he smiled to her, "but I'll be damned if I won't take a short recess." Thus he took the kiss. He hugged her and suddenly he felt the warmth of her body quickly traveling throughout his. He tightly squeezed her and for a moment there, his head speedily spun. "I must go!" he said as he gently pulled apart.

CHAPTER 9

▼

He drove straight to Maria's residence. He had promised her the night. However willfully inclined and honorable his intentions were, a sea of sexual fantasies and unfaithful desires, Moira being the perpetrator, flared in his mind.

"Who says that beauty is in the eyes of the beholder? Moira's beauty was in all the eyes that looked at her!" he just murmured raising his eyes to the rearview mirror to check the back of the car as if Maria were there.

Couldn't blame Moira. Her beauty was not her fault and she did not ask for it. Then in an effort to wipe her off his mind, he forced himself to think of the caller. She told him Peter was his name. He had a strange diction, a cadenza that Moira swore she could recognize.

Perhaps he was the killer. Or maybe he was an accomplice. Or is it possible that he got there late and someone else preceded him to the crime? There was a connection, but it was obscure as a night without stars. A voice, what's a voice without a body? Like in certain movies about invisibility. The actor pretending to be invisible talks and moves freely in a room but one cannot pinpoint the exact position or weather he's standing or sitting. Furthermore one cannot lock up a voice!

Then Paul flashed in his eyes so powerfully he had to blink them to wipe him off. "Mr. Paul Invisible! That's a fucking farce...the whole investigation is a farce. What does Paul have to do with all of this?" he asked to himself, as he was meanwhile entering the Yacht Club. He parked in front of the building, shut the engine and drifted towards the door. He opened it and called her. I thought she was expecting me, he thought. Then he remembered that her car was not in the parking lot and Daisy the little Maltese was not around either.

"Cinderella," he teased her as she stepped in with groceries and wine.

Midnight struck at that moment

"So what are you waiting for? "Go get Daisy in the car!" she commanded him, showing great disposition.

"This mop here needs grooming!" he stated as he returned with Daisy in his arms.

"One of these days I'll get around to it but right now I'm so happy to see you honey that my head is spinning. I thought you left me behind and went off to Italy," she said smiling while she hugged him.

He was restless. He drifted nonchalantly towards the bottle of wine, opened it and filled his glass. Then he asked, "Do you want some?"

"Do I want some? Why are you acting so weird? Since when do you ask? Don't you always fill two glasses?"

Tom smiled and said, "What a creature of habit! Just to break monotony, no? You look hot!" He continued looking steady into her eyes. But at that moment Moira flashed back in his mind's eyes obscuring Maria.

"So quench me!" Maria answered eager to initiate sex.

And so seized by sudden lust Tom grabbed her, swept her off the floor, sat her on the kitchen counter and went for the pulling of her briefs.

"Oh my god, oh my god…" she repeated instantly aroused as if it were her last night of love. However the feline's fury with which he attacked her quickly wore him out.

"Fuck! If I don't calm down," he thought, "I'aint gonna make it!" He took a deep breath and sighed. Seconds later, almost in anger he quickly lift her from the counter and carried her in his arms to the bedroom. He laid her gently on the bed and picked the stereo remote control from the nightstand. He searched and quickly found Rossini's overture, 'William Tell'. Thus he started kissing her and fondling her, filling every pore of her body as the violins and the oboes sweet, smooth, gentle yet intensive rolling sounds filled the emptiness. Maria absorbed it and gave it all. Then, following the flow of the music, he gently penetrated her. She mumbled soft and gentle nonsense words of love and at times deeply and raucously nonsense, in synch with the sonorous moods of the overture. While moaning religious and blasphemous words Tom initiated his rhythmic strokes taken by the crescendo of the piece. Toll of bells, galloping horses, splashing waterfalls, screeching of birds in swarms…all gave him the illusion of a passage through mysterious and exotic dreams.

As the piece flowed towards its height and the kettledrums, tambourines, basses and brass instruments all came together with the frenetic crescendo tremulous strokes of violins' strings to the final organized rumble, Tom initiated his final and brutal marathon of thrusts.

"Harder, harder," she shouted. "Call me slut! Call me whore! Swine! Call me swine…god oh god god…go-o-o-o d."

At her last call for god, thank God, he ran out of thrusts and motionlessly rested upon her body with his head hidden between her neck and the pillow. Then panting as a wounded animal, he slithered from her leaving the palm of his hand over her groins, softly caressing her vagina.

"Oh my God" she whispered, "the energy? Where did you get the energy? I mean you're good at it but God mercy where did you get the energy?"

"Two weeks of abstinence that's where the energy came from!" he murmured and also lied. Moira's sensuality had stimulated him unawarely so that Maria cashed in on the benefits of his renewed long forgotten sexual energy.

However, that night Tom promised to himself to forget Moira. He loved Maria.

The desire for Moira was plain old lust, the male innate animalistic ill-famed libido.

CHAPTER 10

▼

Tom drifted along the corridor with a steady gait and a euphoric look on his face. The elation from the night before lingered still, and the unusual quietness around the co-workers escaped him. Perhaps another time, he would think he had entered a morgue. Head up, shoulders back and chest out as if in the days of the police academy, he didn't acknowledge that the morning's harmony made out of cheering and smiling was of another day.

"Good morning gorgeous!" he said to Loren as if in oblivion, still absorbed within. "Isn't it a beautiful day?"

"Good morning lieutenant!" she responded with a shy and curious smile. Strangely different was the salute he had displayed all of a sudden, she wondered. Not the usual vague salute, which was made out of the waving of four fingers or a gentle knock on the desk as he passed her by.

"By the way, where is everybody?" he asked returning on his steps.

"Everybody was around five minutes ago, sir!"

"So?"

"The chief called them in his office...also the Capt..."

"Bob was called in too?"

"Yes sir!"

"Big trouble ah!" he said almost laughing.

"The chief left orders on this desk that..."

"…I am wanted! Like the fucking western movies, you know, WANTED!" he said, cheerfully still. "Well I guess I must not make him wait."

He was ready. Absorbing complaints was his forte. He had learned throughout growing up that if one was of a mischievous nature, one must learn how to cope with disciplinary action taken from parents, or as in this particular case, from the Chief of Police. Ordering Dan to pick four Uniforms to watchdog Moira round the clock without asking permission was not a small matter.

However, with an air of child's innocence after granting forgiveness for previous little acts of insolence, insolently, he stepped into the chief's office.

"Check that out," he proffered bursting into laughter seeing all of them sitting facing the taciturn superior in a fashionable semicircle. And nobody dared to look at Tom or to join him with laughter. Not discouraged at all, he dared to continue, "The round table of King Arthur and his knights!"

Lots of sour pusses in this room, he then thought. Not even a little lip's twinkle from anybody. Like mannequins condemned to sitting with a stick up the ass to assure total stillness in a showcase.

"Okay! Okay! Here I am," he said to the chief, suddenly with renovated audacity, "Crucify me. Go crucify me! After all I am an apostle of Jesus Christ…isn't my name St. Thomas?"

"You're making this police station a circus. I won't tolerate it." The chief composed said. "Disciplinary actions are on the way unless you comply with the way I interpret law and order. And that goes for all of you also. And let me add that my officers whom you insist on calling Uniforms work for me and they're not puppets on your string."

"Chief, with all do respect Sir, a suspect is in danger. Her life was and is on the line! He seriously affirmed. "It was a necessity and even more than a necessity, a duty. As an officer of the law…my duty…"

"…That young and I'm told beautiful girl, is just fine…"

The captain quickly cut in, "I understand your concern chief. However, we must admit that our investigators here are top of the line…and if Tom felt…"

"…Bob, top of the line or not…top of the line or not," he repeated. He liked that expression. "They must conform, and comply. And that is an order!"

"Of course! But on the human side, although Tom acted irrationally, this Moira needs protection…Tom thinks so and so do I. There are too many intrigues around that young and lovely woman," he said wishing he could have eliminated from his saying, 'lovely woman'."

"Bob, I need my Uniforms, my officers," he quickly corrected fearful to having stimulated laughter, but since nobody dared, he continued. "We have a large city and there isn't enough manpower. Every damn road is either under construction or reconstruction. The snowbirds are back and the motorists speeding fines are way below national quota.

"We must restructure our criteria!" he attempted to look for new words but every thought that entered his mind made him feel argumentative. He had caught himself many times in a situation where he had become argumentative without arguments and afterwards he had regretted it.

"Out of here!" he suddenly burst out. "All of you, I'm loaded with work! Not you Bob! Close the door behind them."

"Ray," the captain said, "for God's sake take it easy on Tom. Give him a little rope."

"I'll take it easy but he has to learn to subordinate. By the way, did he bang that child? What's her name anyhow?" he said with a smirk on his face.

"Moira!"

"What's the story?"

"There's no story, Ray! Tom is a serious cop. He's in love with Maria…"

"When it comes to women, that *I-Italian* doesn't give a damn. He'll screw them even if a dagger were jammed up his ass."

"Yeah! He likes women, don't you?"

"By the way, Bob…I've got me this new babe…"

"I must go!" The captain quickly anticipated getting on his feet. "But I'm coming back to hear all of it, details and all…I mean it. Can leave nothing behind…promise me!"

He went straight to Tom for a quick gossip about the chief. Dan informed him that Tom was out heading to Moira for an emergency that had arisen.

"Dan?" He hesitated.

"Yes sir!"

"How beautiful is this Moira?"

"A bomb shell!" he exclaimed flagging his hands in front of him, drawing in the air with exaggeration, the curvaceous body.

"She's…" and the captain also drew her body in the air with the same exaggeration.

"Do you think Tom…?" he said stopping at that. He, like everybody, also wanted to know if Moira and Tom had consummated their libidos, but couldn't finish the sentence.

"Ask him to come and see me when he comes back…at his convenience," he instead said. Then he drifted towards his office nodding his head.

The bat, assuming it was the murder weapon, had been taken by the coroner. After being examined and reexamined it only showed Moira's old smeared fingerprints. A decadent fiasco indeed! Solid proof that she was at her sister's quickly cleared her. She had not left her sister's house at all for the three days she stayed there. Each one of her sister's neighbors testified that she had spent her time reading on the porch and/or working around the garden. And that suited Tom perfectly. He wanted her uninvolved. He liked her so much.

Jim had found out through asphyxiating researches that a similar killing pattern had taken place in Mobile, Alabama. Peter Dubois, who was arrested as a suspect, managed to escape. He was now fugitive at large on the list of American Most Wanted. Perhaps there was connection. That Peter, the one that telephoned Moira, could be Peter Dubois. And didn't Moira state she would be able to recognize the voice of the caller? And couldn't it then be possible that the caller was indeed Peter Dubois? And perhaps he's hiding in Florida?

The train of suppositions agitated Tom and the nights went sleepless. When he finally did slumber, nightmares followed.

-I'm an investigator and I ought to look at the devil's ass if that is where the assassin has to be found. The reasons that the devil's ass happened to belong to a gorgeous, sensual, full of life young lady should not bother you, because it doesn't bother me. Tom shouted to a man without face that was chasing him armed with shotguns, pistol and grenades.—Shoot me you son of a bitch! Shoot me! Bastard, shoot me so I can prove you're a killer!

The man without face turned out to be the chief's face but before totally vanishing, it faded out as being that of Paul.

It became a matter of fact that every daily event harassed him into ghastly and ghostly nightmares. Grotesque faces on deformed bodies, with an arsenal of firearms harnessed around their members, appeared menacingly aiming at him. And at the end of every nightmare he jumped up to a sudden sitting position. While sitting in a sea of sweat, he would mutter stressed out words of nonsense.

But his stress ended at the same moment he jumped in the shower. Then and only then, his rejuvenated gut feelings returned intact. The usual relentless stamina to pursue a suspect was also revamped. In fact he made contact with Mobile's agency and had the forensic authority send in tapes of Peter Dubois' recorded voice and photos.

Once that was done Tom walked straight to the captain's office and just said, as a matter of fact, "I need a moment of your time. Please listen. We have reason to believe that there is a connection between the crimes here and those in Alabama!"

He then, after a moment of silence, looked at the dumbfounded captain and continued, "I'm totally convinced that the man that called Moira is the serial killer Peter Dubois. And Moira will help us identify that voice when Jim reconstructs whatever unusual sound of voice she's talking about. In addition, my instincts tell me Dubois could be hanging around Florida, perhaps in Miami. The similarity of these two cases are point-for-point incredibly credible. Of course a copycat could result from our investigation also. Not ignoring our local events I ask permission to carry on. Our detectives are now looking into a few cases of sexually abused children, male and female, ex-friends of the ex-priest. In fact we've just ended an interrogation with a fellow that Sean molested many years ago."

The captain listened and took it all in while shaking his head as Tom kept on talking, "Andrea, the Rabbi's wife, has been interrogated persistently. We have found large deposits in different banks and the names of her lovers. They are now under investigations. Unfortunately, all of them, and they were more than a few, are just lover boys. Insignificant boys who couldn't cut an apple with a knife, never mind puncturing the Rabbi's chest with an oyster dagger like a colander. As for Moira, she's been proved innocent..."

"Carry on Tom. Carry on and keep me informed. I'll ask the chief to give you a little extra rope. Good luck!

CHAPTER 11

When Tom walked through the corridor with Moira by his side heading to Jim's wired-room, the eyes of the Uniforms, men and women, jumped out of their orbits. The men, of course, tilted their heads to the right and quickly to the left following the rhythmical oscillation of her body's curves.

Dan, Phil and Gianni stood next to each other in a corner, unsuccessfully trying to look preoccupied. Loren dropped her mouth for an indeterminate length of time. It took the usual Tom's thud on the desk with his knuckles to snap her out. The introduction of Moira to Jim belonged to a funny movie's funny episode. His usual bunch of jumping wires that lived in him, instead of his nervous system, froze. Then, avoiding direct contact with Moira's eyes, he mumbled a few confused sentences that had lost their meanings even before were spoken.

Moira giggled.

Once the short but intense commotion subdued, it was time to work.

Moira sat pensive and nervous before the first tape, throwing a quick glance here and there. Then she threw her warm melancholic eyes at Tom, generating enough heat, to set him on fire.

He shook is head.

Then he smiled at her with comforting paternal attempts and quickly handed her Dubois's photos.

"Please, take a good look at them!"

No recollection at all and no resemblance to anyone she knew. But something about Dubois's eyes suddenly hit Tom.

Intense, profound, mysterious! Cut gloriously large with rolled up pupils hidden halfway into the sockets. Dubois, if Tom was the super detective that he thought of himself, had a surgical change of face; a total different physiognomy to camouflage his identity. But can the depth of one's eyes, the form, the mellowness or strength, be altered? Impossible. Mirrors of souls they are! Besides new techniques concerning eyes were available to prove identification.

Fastidiously as it was to look at Jim at work, Tom felt comfortable. Jim was magic with his apparatus of electronic devices. However nobody, especially Tom, could cut in when he was on a new task. And this task was of an overwhelming entity.

He nervously twisted and jumped like a sack filled with springs, then was adrift at times. Then he leaped in full control around the arsenal of transmitters, receivers and transporters. In command of the whole electronic system, he meticulously split, connected and reconnected the sounds of vowels and consonants in search of a definite foreign, domestic, fake or camouflaged accent. Jim should be working for the FEDs with CIA, but Tom was not going to share him. He was too valuable.

Tom had learned during the time of the investigation to understand his small group of detectives. How efficient they were pursuing their task. However, at times he teased them and sarcastically so just the same. With Jim, however, when he was at work, and specifically in this particular time, and during the splitting of vowels and consonants to create one specific tone of voice, he did not dare. Who could? Jim was a species of his own. The only person the kid allowed near him was Loren with the delivery of a cup of coffee at the bottom of every working hour. And Loren's visit lasted but a minute, for Jim drank his coffee with a bestial speed and avidity.

That pleased Loren just the same. It was refreshing for a change to deliver coffee to someone other than Tom, who never drank it. Besides, it was also refreshing for her not to meet Tom's eyes, which clearly but unexplainably, made her ill at ease.

That day Tom felt calm and confident being next to Moira. He waited patiently for Jim to adjust the last few details and then put the tapes in operational modes.

"All is in perfect order," he happily announced.

"Start the first tape!" Tom said while Moira sat and waited pensively yet anxious to hear the tape.

At the first few words Moira turned to Tom and just said, "No way! This isn't the voice I know!"

"Please!" he softly spoke, "Listen to the whole tape!"

She nodded her head and continued to listen. When the tape ran out she positively pronounced: "It's not!"

"Are you sure? Do you want to listen again?"

"I'm positive! Tom! I'm positive!" she cried.

"Okay, no need to get upset. Either you recognize or not, any of the voices on tapes, we do appreciate just the same that you're helping us."

"I'm sorry, I feel weird...it's eerie!"

"Do you want coffee?" he asked her but the fact was he wanted one and this time perhaps he would drink it.

"No thanks!"

"Okay! Do you want to listen to the other tape or..."

"Yes!" She quickly cut in.

"No! It's not his voice," she stopped listening at the first few words. "It's not. God, Tom I'm so sorry, I'm so sorry...maybe I can't tell...I'm so sorry."

"Loren!" he almost shouted opening the door, "Please two coffees!"

"Excuse me," Jim proffered.

"Three...three coffee," he fully shouted this time.

After Loren left, Tom sat down next to Moira as she gently sipped her coffee. He put his arm around her glorious shoulders and softly spoke, "Baby," as if they were lovers for the eternity. "It doesn't matter if you don't recognize it, your help still is an overwhelming effort. The mere fact that I took you away from your daily routine..."

"I'm so sorry Tom! I wish...I think...maybe my head plays tricks on me. I really thought I could help you!

"Okay, okay, it doesn't matter, baby! You did help. You are helping...We can postpone this ordeal to another day!"

"No! Tom please I want to finish the job! I do want to listen to the last tape!"

"Start the last tape, please," Tom pleaded.

Jim didn't move. So intent he was listening to him speaking softly, gently with so much tenderness to Moira. What was happening to his tough lieutenant? A man he respected for his strong will, as well as other strengths. He tenderly spoke to Moira, fondly, with loving care, sincerely, without affectation.

"Please start the last tape," Tom simply asked again.

And that voice burst into Moira's ears with the same cacophonic disgrace as the produced note of a violinist's off-key to the ears of a symphony's director.

"That's it! That's the voice!" she shouted jumping into Tom's arms laughing and crying while he held her tighter onto him incapable to let go.

Tom had the voice. And for that it took an electronic freak like Jim to split into three different dialects on three different tapes. But as for the face, Tom was still in the dark. A surgically changed face was impossible for them to return to the original, which left Tom at impossible odds, Dubois's voice and eyes. An assumption, of course, which augmented instead of lessening his existing doubts. Nevertheless he tortured himself to study Dubois's eyes on the photographs under magnifying glasses. Deeply rooted into his sockets, the black pupils embroidered with yellow dots spitted out signs of horror, satire, hate and hidden mystery.

CHAPTER 12

———————▼———————

Lieutenant St. Thomas, needed rest and some fresh air, and the beach that day looked promising. He drove to the parking lot, locked the car and purposely ignored the meter. The sea at Lake Worth beach was at its highest splendor.

"My beautiful little creatures, I want you to know that you're my favorite *people*," he said to the sandpipers tiptoeing away from the thin frothy lips of the gentle waves that bathed the sand.

What a sense of peace, of tranquility and solitude.

However, he wanted company, someone to talk to. To have lunch, perhaps with Dan, or perhaps with Gianni, Phil or even Jim; that crazy kid with a bundle of jumping wires in place of a nervous system. No! Not with the captain, and definitely not with the chief!

No! That wouldn't cut it. Unintentionally, but surely their conversation would fall on the investigations. Perhaps Maria would be the most suitable candidate? No Maria was off limits! He'd feel guilty! Guilty? Why guilty? About Moira, perhaps! But there was nothing going on there! There was no consummation there! Who says a man cannot desire a woman other than his own? Yes, lust was there, but he managed to keep his sanity. Or was it insanity not to take advantage of that blissful occasion?

"Catch the moment! What a nut!" he heard himself saying.

No! Maria's love was real. He could touch it. No, no doubts! Tom St. Thomas felt that love. He could touch that love and believed it, like St. Thomas touched Jesus' wounds and cuts and believed He was the Son of Man.

However, he felt the desire for Moira was under his skin. Lust drove him crazy. Night after night, lain in bed with his eyes stuck at the ceiling, he thought of her. Damned! It was not real but a mere trick of sexual fantasy.

The nights went sleepless.

And God knows if he needed his sleep!

Killers…thinking of killers also interfered with the best part of his few hours of sleep and Moira deprived him of the remaining few.

It was lust he was after not love.

Relentlessly that thought persecuted him, like he relentlessly persecuted killers.

"Go for it!"

One inner voice spoke to him.

"Lay off!"

Said the other.

But the following day he arranged to meet with her. Granted they were innocent little rendezvous that accomplished little. But to see her and talk to her made him feel good inside and he needed that.

As the investigation drew near the final moment, he sat apart the meetings allowing only short conversations over the phone.

It excited him to hear her voice, the excitement she put into every word. However, 'It is the woman that chooses the man that will choose her' he had once read and agreed with the maker of the statement, and Maria had chosen him to choose her before Moira.

And that was just about it!

It was an easy infatuation for Moira. She had never met a man like Tom; strong, pleasant looking, sure of himself, who when clear of doubts he turned commanding. Yet, he also was sympathetic, understanding, alert, quick and earnest. And among of all that, she saw in his languid yet sparkling eyes, in the smile as that of an adolescent, in the fine looking face and in the almost fragile small body an inner energy that could have lit the Empire State building!

CHAPTER 13

$\blacktriangledown$

The Minister's will was clear and short; Moira had the house and half a million. The rest of the Minister's money had mysteriously disappeared. The fat bank accounts had been closed the day before he was murdered. The whole damn affair made no sense at all. The bankers were summoned up and interrogated. All said, he was alone while making withdrawal.

They also cleared Moira. She had neither withdrawn nor deposited money from his account. Never!

Gianni substituted Dan and Phil to investigate Andrea, the Rabbi's wife.

Tom's decision rose from the fact that being young, blue eyed and with a mop of wavy black hair cascading to his shoulders over a powerful body, he would have easy access to her confidence. However she turned out innocent on all accounts like Moira.

Andrea didn't mind the switch. It suited her just right to meet with that handsome boy and she didn't bat an eye when he got rough with her. On the contrary, his anger to her evasive answers about a current lover excited her. Cautiously, under heavy questioning she finally admitted that there was a prospect in the air but she succeeded in keeping her distance.

"A prospect in the air? But you've succeeded in keeping your distance! And, of course, I bet you expect me to believe you."

"I'm not what you're making of me. I was a faithful and a good wife for many years. My husband, although religious, was also a brutal man and nasty!"

"Why do you feel you have to justify wrongdoing to me? I'm here to interrogate and investigate you, not to hear your confessions."

She didn't answer that.

"Perhaps…" she murmured. "Perhaps I need to focus on my life, on who I really am."

Possibly her statements were sincere but Gianni didn't buy it. Who was she kidding? He felt she was attracted to him big time and made no secret of it. Indeed his continental flair, strength, intelligence and savoir-fare could feverishly attract a woman. However, Gianni kept his distance. Not that she didn't turn him on, indeed she did. However, the lieutenant had been specific in his recommendations to them.

"Avoid relations of any kind with a suspect of the opposite sex."

They were, of course, aware of his liking Moira. However, there was no reason to believe they had consummated their libido.

Tom strolled around the beach with a slow pace. His usual gait was gone. It didn't matter. He wasn't walking to get physical exercise. It was his head that needed a tune up. Adrift at the edge of the sea he kicked the gentle wave that wet his feet. And when he noticed the sandpipers gently tiptoeing away from the sprinkling he had caused, he murmured with a smile, "sorry little fellas."

He walked north passing the Hilton, and the chain of other waterfront hotels. He stopped at the Four Seasons. He thought of the exquisite lunches and the few dinners he had enjoyed there. Going in crossed his mind. His wardrobe, his sandy and wet feet stopped him. He smiled and murmured, "they'll stop me at the door!" Or perhaps they'll think he is a pauper and give him a bowl of soup. Then suddenly he turned back on his steps heading towards the pier. After a few minutes of hesitation, he closed in. He stopped at the three steps that led to the ramp and slowly put his loafers on, and then steadfastly walked to the ticket booth.

"Lieutenant SanTommaso? Long time no see…" greeted the familiar yet, arrogant voice, from the pitch-dark corner of the booth that resembled a chicken coop.

"Paul?" he called trying to clearly see the dark figure standing in the obscurity. "I knew you lived in the dark, but that dark?" he joked laughing as Paul approached him.

"I saw you coming and headed to play hide and seek."

"What's going on?"

"Same bull, same bull…perhaps you have a lot to tell me. How is…?"

"Stop right there, Paul! No talk about my work. Don't spoil it! I have two more hours of leisure before resuming," he smiled.

"I'm impressed!" Paul also smiled. "I didn't think you were capable of letting go…"

"Letting go? Shit! I was talking about a few hours…"

"I didn't think so! So we'll join the mute people."

"No, but you can join me for lunch at John G's if you promise to keep the conversation on the light side. But I see that…"

"You see nothing Tom. Let's go! Hey loser" he shouted to the guy inside. "I'll see you when I see you!" Then he jumped over the counter, stepped in front of Tom and with a big smile on his face said, "I'm all yours Tom!"

During repast the conversation was indeed on the carefree side, Tom laughed at Paul's few extravagant phrases.

"One of these days when you're done finding the killer…"

"What makes you believe the killer is one…"

"Don't miss a shot, *signor tenente*! Sort of saying! But at any rate as I was saying before you interrupted me, one of these days I'll treat you to one of my favorite restaurants!" Paul smiling concluded.

It was time to bid goodbye. But Tom hesitated a bit before leaving. While looking in his eyes, only imagining the center point of them for the dark pitch lenses totally eclipsed he asked, "Do you ever consider removing them?"

"Not on your life. I sleep with them. See you Tom! You're a real pain in the ass…"

Time had gone so fast that as he left Paul, he felt robbed of his simple yet peaceful lunch.

As he put his foot in his office, Tom, not aware of the why, called Loren in. She, as usual, felt prickly. She couldn't help it. There was something about him that disturbed her and Tom was aware of it. Although she must admit he was always pleasant and kind to her. Perhaps it was the way he scrutinized people and things. She had caught him many times in his office, during the notorious delivery of coffee, cradling and turning over and over any meaningless object in his hand. With his glasses on the tip of his nose, he seemed to study the details of it, as if immortality were to be found there. And she caught him more than a few times, quickly running his eyes over her body from head to toe as if he wanted to be sure her anatomy was synchronized with the laws of gravity.

She stepped in empty handed but quickly said, "I'm sorry I'll make you coffee!"

"Never mind! Come in please. Have a seat."

Again she felt those melancholic eyes on her anatomy making her blood rush to her face to the point of sensing levitation. However, she quickly sat before takeoff.

"I have the impression that, although I do not know why, you feel intimidated by me." He simply said with an encouraging smile while his eyes, as for a miracle, sparkled of joviality and tenderness. "If I'm doing or saying something that is causing that, please make me aware. I promise you I'll correct it."

"No sir...I..."

"By the way I do have a name...we're not in Italy here where a doctor must be called: dottore, a lawyer: avvocato, a professor: professore, a lieutenant: tenente. We're a family here! Out there with other authorities perhaps sir or lieutenant is just fine but here...I feel we're family. Tom, Tom will be just fine!"

"Okay, "she murmured with a shy smile.

"Now let's rehearse it," he said with a chuckle, "Loren can I have my coffee?"

"Yes sir! Yes Tom. Regular?" She asked returning the chuckle, while she got up.

"No! It's not necessary."

"Yes it is, Tom. The rehearsal ain't over. From now on I must make sure to brew it the way you like it!" she promptly responded with a smile, feeling easiness never felt before!

Tom laughed.

An icebreaker it was and the laughter assured the melting.

Achievement of freedom of his senses! For some reason he found himself clumsy in direct confrontation with her. And on her part she couldn't believe that his saying and his ways of looking at her no longer caused her to blush. On the contrary later on as he saluted her on his way to his office, or sometimes when she was totally absorbed in her paperwork, he naughtily startled her with a sharp knock of his knuckles on her desk. Or just by waving a few fingers at a distance, all that attention, which once would have altered her usual calm disposition, now raised the level of her senses.

The woman in her made her think how charming he really was. Why hadn't she seen it before? "Perhaps," she reasoned, "it was the position he held and the austerity that he was so naturally embedded."

Tom dismissed her for the time being, but a few days after, seeing her so joyful, caught the occasion to invite her back to his office for a chat.

"Have a seat!" he said scrutinizing her body as usual. "May I ask you a simple question?"

"Shoot! Surely shoot!"

"Does Paul ever take his dark glasses out during you know what?"

"I don't give him a chance," she replied bursting into laughter taking Tom along. But after the laughter, with a serious tone of voice she said, "Why do I think...I mean, I get the impression you're thinking he's a suspect? Is he?"

Tom raised his shoulders. He looked deeply in her eyes and, without intimidation whatsoever he proffered, "In the eyes of a true detective everybody is a suspect until proven the contrary..."

"Even I..." she responded.

"The captain! Even the chief!" he heartily laughed.

As the conversation was just about to pick up momentum, Dan showed up at the door with his usual classic moment of hesitation.

"Okay shoot!"

"Sorry! Didn't mean to disturb you. Two big boys...FBI! You're wanted at the chief's..."

"WANTED! That word was his first learned English word, when he was in Italy. Still a young boy he scraped cents from everybody's close to him to buy the ticket for the western movies he loved so much, which he called cowboys movies. And that 'WANTED' was posted everywhere.

CHAPTER 14

▼

"Tom, come in!" said the chief as Tom peeped inside. Contrary to his wretched attitude towards Tom because of his unruly conduct, the chief found himself at his best. He evidently was on the path to impress the two fellows sitting across him.

Tom knew them both. He exchanged an ironic and conspiratorial smile with the slender and well-dressed character. They met years back at a conference in Washington DC.

Tom was then a new lieutenant freshly smelling of Police academy and Danny a new FBI agent freshly smelling of FBI academy. As their eyes met a rapport began. They smelled each other at once. At the end of the first sitting that day, Danny approached Tom and said, "Lieutenant…St. Thomas, correct? If you're willing to skip the afternoon's session, I know of an Italian restaurant in Georgetown that would clear out boredom."

"Who says I was going to attend?" Tom answered with a nonchalantly shrug of his shoulders and a smile.

"Then it's a deal. I like that…"

On the way out of the hotel, he led him to a taxicab.

"Uncle Sam has procured a taxicab for us. Allow me to offer you a spin." Danny said with an arrogant smile.

"Us from small towns agencies don't have the luxury of Uncle Sam's pecuniary extravagance."

"Where are you heading from here?" he asked, choosing a more direct approach.

"For now back to Connecticut, indeed, Hartford, at least for a few years, to make my bones. However, to southeast Florida as soon as openings are available. I'm hoping for Palm Beach County, any town!"

"You also could take advantage of Uncle Sam's pecuniary extravagance!"

"How is that?"

"Join us? You know, the big guys from the Federal Agency! I can get you on board in no time at all. I've got important connections." he smiled. "That's a lie. The truth is my boss spotted you and sent me to bribe you..." he now contagiously laughed.

"I thought your scouting was genuine."

"But of course, I pointed you out to him. I didn't want to sound arrogant and look flamboyant in your eyes. Your analytical shrewdness of people makes me ill at ease. I saw you scrutinizing everything and everybody since you stepped in." he said smiling. "At any rate, 'I like his suit,'" he answered me after he looked you up.

"Permission to carry on granted! By the way, bribe him if you have to!" were his last words to me.

"I see! However, you should warn your boss that bribes are punishable in a court of law. At any case, they're not favorable within the law!"

"Perhaps you're right! But the FBI does go to the extreme to achieve end results of things."

"Hey, thanks for the offer, but after Connecticut I want my sun. I was born in a warm climate and I want to die in a warm climate.

As the chief was enumerating tips and leads and, of course, went all out to praise Tom's great work, Danny shook his head in approval. But flashes of when he first met Tom interfered with the chief's information. Moreover, he wanted to be one on one with Tom and perhaps get into a serious talk about the investigation. But since the chief wasn't coming up for air with his nonsense, Danny cut him short.

"We're going to stick around for awhile and we can go over again," he firmly stated. "For now the lieutenant here will find us a place to stay and perhaps we'll get in touch with you tomorrow. We're here to give a hand if necessary."

"A hand my ass," Tom thought.

Danny knew the type. Tom would share but only little bits of information. He had studied him well during lunch at that glorious restaurant in Georgetown. He was jealous of his task and not for any power gains. Didn't take Danny any length of time to find out the kind of paste Tom was made of.

"Free of all kind of nonsense and glory, his job, for whatever it was worth, was his glory."

"Do you think you can find a decent place to have dinner later on?" Danny asked outside of the chief's office, "And perhaps after you're done with the bullshit that's going on around here, you'll consider joining us; you know, the big guys. My boss is a stubborn man. He can accept the first no for an answer but doesn't cope too well with the second refusal."

"Please, I'm in tears. I'm an emotional creature. Tell your boss, I wouldn't last but a day."

"You're wasted here!" he said with the usual FBI agents' cool arrogance.

"Don't get me wrong. I feel honored. I do have…well, feelings you know."

"No kidding?"

"Thank your boss for me but I love it here," he said with a smirk. "I love the fucking hot temperature, the beaches and the bitches, and the stupidity that surrounds us all. I love the chief with all his fucking nonsense. And mostly, I love my small group of detectives. However, never let it slip, they think I hate them…" he burst into a sonorous laughter taking Danny and his partner along.

"Okay! Promise! I'll never ask you again! How is the captain?" he suddenly asked.

"Bob? He's legit! Influenced a bit by the chief but in the end he comes to his senses.

"Of course you and I agree that we're dealing with a serial killer…"

"In the sense that the crimes were committed by the same killer, yes! Otherwise we're not in agreement!"

"Specifically?"

"Specifically this is not the usual bloodthirsty killer. He's not the usual Joe-Blow. Not a sniper type either. This one is after big money. A parenthesis, I wouldn't be surprised if his fourth victim were under his scrupulous study. Since we have little to go on, I have this half idea that he believes his crimes were perfect. All indications show that the three victims were not taken at random. The killer, I'm guessing one-man show, chose them because they were millionaire. He chose them because of the big money, logically, methodically, systematically with plenty of premeditation. Eliminated, for disguise, by different weapons within the timeframe of two or three hours. In English they were studiously organized and reorganized assassinations. As for the record, three million were withdrawn from each bank account. Nine million in all, the amount of the Florida single week lotto price. Furthermore, with the advantage of no claim from the IRS mind you. The bankers provided proof that each victim took the money three hours before being done in, which confuses the investigation. The victims knew the killer. Acquaintances, perhaps, he or she had easy access to their residences. Bribes, extortions, anything of that sort; you do your homework on that. Withdrawals were voluntary, nevertheless one must assume they didn't reckon they were going to end up at the morgue."

"Yeah, I did follow and thought so too. However, for what I've read in the coroner report and the nothingness from the forensic whiz kids, there's little if anything at all to go on."

"Lots of tips, lots of interrogations without serious suspects!"

"Do you need a hand? Do you want us to stick around?"

"Danny, don't you charge Uncle Sam enough money for classy dinners and expensive wines within the timeframe of working hours? While here there isn't too much to do for you." he smiled with innuendo. "I would love to spend some time together but I'm loaded with work. You know the sheriff is on my case, along with all the other existing fucking agencies in the county."

"By the way, why did you turn down the interview with Paula Zhan?"

"I have no serious information to release to her. I would have loved to. Nice ass!" he said smiling. "As for general information, the chief was plastered with tons of makeup the few times he stood in front of the camera. And every time after that he called me in his office with one excuse or another asking me if I liked the way he looked live on camera."

"How did he look?" Danny smiled.

"I never saw the clips, but told him he looked as good as an actor…he's a better actor than the so assumingly 'professionals' anyhow! Talent! He's got talent! He performs daily in his office and we're all his supporting actors or better yet his doubles. Evidently he missed his vocation!" Tom burst into laughter until tears came out of his eyes consequently affecting Danny and his partner whose laughter also caused tears.

"My offer still stands." he said after catching one tear with his index finger before running down his cheek.

"I'm sure! But I like his acting…I like the chief! He is the nicest guy, don't come any nicer. But he has no concept of crimes and that suits me just fine!"

"You're impossible!"

"And you're a pain in the ass! Get it through your skull, I'm not leaving Florida!"

"Can we change subject?"

"Gladly!"

"May I ask you a personal question?"

"Sure, as long as it is not about my coffee that I never drink." he said with a wise smile.

"What's your political orientation?" he went straight to the point.

"Are we allowed to have one?"

"You're a citizen of the United States, are you not?" he took a kidding approach.

"Naturalized, meaning…"

"I do know what it means…"

"Are you trying to ask me if I like Bush?"

"Basically!"

"Well okay! Promise me that you'll not be offended no matter what and I'll throw the sac open…"

"Throw it open!"

"This Bush...I'm not going to call him names. You might resent it. After all you work for him."

"Don't you?"

"Perhaps but not as directly!"

"You're funny!"

Like father like son! They initiate new jobs before they accomplish old ones. He would have smelled like a rose if had finished the job in Afghanistan and captured Bin Laden. He wanted him 'Dead or Alive!'"

"A Texas rancher! What do expect?" he let the comment go unintentionally. He didn't mean to unveil his own orientation to Tom. Didn't cut it with FBI's criteria.

"Runs in the family! Like the father 'Read my lips...' At any rate the son's duty was to capture Bin if it meant to flatten all the mountains and bury him under his shelter."

"Are you telling me it was wrong of him to start a war in Iraq?"

"Damned right it was!"

"What about the weapons of mass destruction?"

"Later on perhaps, given the benefit of the doubt!" he said now a bit agitated.

"Perhaps he had no choice..."

"Do you what to talk about criminals? Our nation's political criminals?" Tom was now blazing."

"No! I get my paycheck next week!" he answered with a faded smile.

It was the first time the lieutenant talked politics. He had always avoided conversation about religious or political issues. He thought it was nonsense. Most people he knew sailed on the troubled issues with a plethora of misconceptions. Navigating in a circle like a ship that lost the rudder! Never approach the issues with due respect and sincerity!

They wrongly choose power games!

Profit and convenience, selfishness and self-growth!

CHAPTER 15

▼

As much as Tom liked Danny and as much as he was getting used to his partner, he became distraught when he heard that the big boys' superior had ordered them not to abandon the region yet. Thus an accommodation for projects and paperwork was given to them within the police station's premises. Although he considered his friend's attempts benign, Tom let no one directly interfere with the ongoing investigations which sort of forced Danny to spend a lot of time with the captain.

From him he was fed the pros and cons.

"Tom? Perhaps he's crazy, full of his Italian gaps. However he's still one of the best in our business. Unfortunately, in these particular cases, the killer or killers have left no evidence whatsoever. Nothing! Not a stain of blood, not a fingerprint, no shoes print not even a trace of tires on the driveways. The pedophile choked to death with a left electrical and mechanical prosthetic arm left us all empty handed. Only fingerprints on the bat that smashed the minister's face belonged to Moira, but were antique, as antique as Methuselah. Moira's alibi stands strongly against all other evidences, if there even were any. She's a sweet creature who as you already know helped us identify the voice of the fugitive, Dubois, the man with a plastic face according to Tom. It all sounds crazy and as strange as it may sound I'm starting to believe like Tom this asshole had his face surgically redone after he escaped from the hands of Mobile's police. Tom's assumptions that Dubois may be hanging around Florida are also believable."

Then suddenly, corrupted by Moira's image that clearly and strongly flashed in his mind, he without forewarning just said, "If you have the misfortune…misfortune in a male point of view, to meet Moira, you'll never forget her!"

"Meaning?"

"Her beauty!"

"There is a rumor going on…isn't there?" Danny said anxious to get the full story of the rumor that Tom was infatuated up his ass with Moira.

And the captain fell for it all the way.

"Well…although he is in love with his fiancée Maria…well during investigation…well…Tom totally lost it for a while. Not affecting, of course, the way he conducted the whole investigation with rigor and intelligence."

Danny shook his head and kept his silence for a while. Then he proffered, "I know Tom! We met in Washington a few years back and we sort of smelled each other, you know? I am well aware of his straight conduct. Or you may say professionalism, but a woman can twist or change a man's decisions and his views…especially if the bed is good, don't you think?"

"No! I mean yes! Of course! In most cases! But Tom was capable of separating his feelings from his duty. I followed up on that on a daily basis. And I've personally checked Moira's alibi. It is so strong that if she turns out to be the killer she would deserve to go free for being a mastermind of crimes," smiled the captain.

Danny was listening attentively but shaking his head. Then he wondered how beautiful she must be. It seemed that when Moira's name first came about, everybody in the station appeared smiling and radiant. "How beautiful is she?" he asked. And suddenly, he let himself be overwhelmed by a great desire to meet her.

The captain read Danny's thoughts. "She's mafia's staff!" he said, perhaps not so jokingly, with innuendo.

"I hear you!" Danny promptly responded.

"Basically, although it is hard to believe, I do believe Tom's determination to find the face that belong to the voice may just about happen. And that will get us closer to our local case! Amen!"

CHAPTER 16

▼

"Angelo, Lieutenant St. Thomas, Tom you know? How are you?"

"Fine! Lieutenant, what can I do for you," the owner of Paradiso Ristorante answered. "A quite table for a party of two?"

"Party of three, this time. Is it possible?"

"How can I say no to you, lieutenant…I'm not a suspect I hope…" he laughed.

And his old saying that everybody is a suspect until proven otherwise made him smile within. But he ignored the comment. Instead he asked, "Tonight at eight, is that good for you?"

It was good and at eight sharp, Tom, Danny and his partner walked in.

They were at the last bite when Dan called, again with his classic hesitation. "Do you have a minute?"

"Shoot Dan! Hold on! Someone is trying to reach me."

It was Gianni, with the same bad news, and again Jim called and then Phil…

"Okay!" he said to Phil with a tread of voice. Then he clicked back to Dan.

"Name, address and I'll be on my way. I will meet all of you there." Then turning to Danny he murmured, "Are you coming? According to Dan there's similarity to the other three cases. This time where the rich, and sometimes rich and famous, have summer mansions, Palm Beach or Fantasy Island like some flamboyant newspaperman calls it."

Meanwhile he put a gentle hand on Reno, the waiter, asking for the check.

Danny pushed Tom's Master Card under his hand and seriously said, "Uncle Sam will take care of it as he pulled his card out. You do deserve it. Go! I'll meet you there! Go! I'll get the exact address from your guys.

"Leave him a lavish tip. Reno is a good guy!" Then humoring himself for it might be long time before laughing again, he continued, "It's not your money anyhow!"

Quickly and without commotion, Tom showed up at the premises before everybody else. Then he heard the blast of the sheriff's siren drawing near.

"Fuck!" he murmured. Tom knew he was not within his jurisdiction. However getting to the crime scene before other agencies was not a felony, as far as he was concerned.

The sheriff arrogantly walked in. He purposely ignored Tom and went straight to the dead body. He looked over the victim with disdain and disbelief. He finally acknowledged Tom's presence and sarcastically remarked, "Lieutenant Tommasso, did you, shall we say, premeditate this event so you can document it and add it to your other crime files? I don't remember giving orders to my chopper pilot to fly you over! Is it possible I have a spy within my agency?"

Tom suddenly had an attack of blood flooding his brain. The adrenaline, which had already signaled loss of temperance, ran over the limits of his tolerance. However, with overwhelming effort to restrain anger, he said, "Sheriff I get these nasty vibes that you don't like me and since I'm not here to win a Beauty Contest I really don't give a fuck…"

"Easy, easy Lieutenant…"

"…Lieutenant my ass!" he cut him short. The effort to control his temper abandoned him and with eyes spitting fire he admonished, "Get it through your fucking redneck skull that your sarcasm doesn't cut it with me. Try again and I'll stick the barrel of my gun up your ass and, puff, scatter your guts around."

"You're totally out of control and out of your jurisdiction my boy! You don't talk to me like that. And you have no reason to be here!"

"I'm an investigator and if someone shoots you on the way to your graveyard do you really think I give a fuck if it is within my jurisdiction? Or do you think I'm going to wait outside your tombstone waiting for your fat-ass uniforms to bring you a flower? So let me state once and for all, do your thing and I'll do mine."

"Peace and collaboration is what I'm looking for," the sheriff stated with a sudden change of heart omitting sarcasm.

"I have no problem with that but keep in mind that I want no more of your bullshit. And by the way, my name is St. Thomas, you know, spelled exactly like Jesus Christ's apostle. Or you can call me Tom, if you wish, but never Tommasso or St Tom! If you want peace we'll collaborate. We'll share notes and forensic reports. If war is what you're looking for, I've already told you where your guts will end up."

There was a moment of silence, between the two of them and not to rewrite the speech for the victim's eulogy. Danny, his partner, and Gianni walked in to break the still moment. Danny quickly flashed his FBI badge to both of them to conceal his acquaintance with Tom to the sheriff. The anger on Tom's face showed clearly that a dispute over the case had been going on before the arrival of other investigators from both agencies.

Meanwhile Tom was blaspheming in his mind; same damn style! And certainly the same killer! One more tormented episode to feed his nightly nightmares. Not a smidgen of anything to go by. The guru, impaled on the wall by seven arrows like a San Sebastian, lived alone in a sumptuous palace with its retro façade looking at the Atlantic Ocean. Although they all collected items for possible evidence, Tom felt there weren't any incriminatory possibilities!

The blood from the seven wounds was still warm and was dripping in a bloody pool around his feet. It obliterated the continuity of the splendid ceramic tiles' design. No contamination of other agents was evident. Once gain, there was nothing to go by. No evidence of any sort! And as far as the money goes the killer, whom Tom believed being the same that assassinated the other three religious men, was climbing the ladder of wealth. And that proved him right when going over the guru's assassination, Tom found out that the amount of the bounty was taken out of the banks by the victim himself. So testified the bankers. And again like the others this victim, also, opened the doors to his own death. No broken windows, no broken doors, no forced entrance of any kind. Tom theory was beginning to hold water yet it leaked fiercely.

"One must assume," he murmured to Danny a few days later, while he sat on the other side of the desk, "that the killer is a friend, a lover, a companion, a sister, a brother, a son, or even a motherfucker mother?" Then as if Danny wasn't there, he continued talking. It was a pattern that altered his rationality during rare but often enough sudden attacks of an irrational state of monomania.

"Come down," Danny cautioned him. "Perhaps, I should ask the chief to give you a couple of weeks off…go to the Bahamas with Maria and let the chief and the captains worry about it all."

"Fuck the Bahamas! I'll find him, her…them! I have a few things I must tell him, her…them, before I lock him, her…them up!"

This fuck, Danny thought, concealing a smile. He's so out of the ordinary, so eccentric, he's a born FBI agent.

It was pointless. Everybody annoyed Tom even Danny. Perhaps he, more than everybody else with that air of superman, 'the big guy from the federal agency'. He had said before leaving the crime scene, "I'm going to stick around," as if without him life in southeast Florida will go wasted. And since his mind had gone on a roller coaster of thoughts between opening events and closing dilemmas, his last acquaintance, the sheriff, flashed in his head. It was that damned southern drawl he could not stomach, he could not tolerate. If he knew rednecks as he knew rednecks the sheriff was the epitome of its class.

He was not going to budge.

"Lieutenant St. Thomas," he murmured, switching the train of thoughts on the way to his apartment leaving his office, "You must go to see Maria. It's a must! That poor and sweet creature can no longer be ignored no matter how indulgent your work is."

Thus furiously, he made a U turn towards Maria's apartment when seven arrows insistently flashed in and out of his mind. Drawings of hearts pierced by a bunch of arrows were persistently entering and leaving his mind. He shook his head and for an instant all vanished. Just for an instant, for that vision reappeared more consistently as if it were brooding inside of him for quite a while. Then he heard himself saying, "A bunch? For God's sake! There were not a bunch. They were seven! I counted! Where? Where did I see the drawing?"

Having no recollection of where he saw the drawing he just murmured, "What does that prove? Drawings with piercing hearts were part of my childhood; *Cristi, Madonne* and *coglioni d'ogni ceto* (Christs, Madonnas and blockheads of all ranks!)

Latent, the old nine yards is miserably resting in a latent stage. Difficult! Of course crimes are difficult to solve but one lead leads to another and 'boom', everything falls into place.

Amid all the train of thought, with innumerable visions, he made another skidding U turn. Oblivious of his determination to go to Maria, he drove to his apartment.

A sound night of sleep will wipe off those relentless thoughts and visions!

CHAPTER 17

▼

Once again Tom tossed about in his bed in a sea of sweat. The annoying agitation mitigated by sudden moments of slumber tranquillized him a bit. But as he opened his eyes the restlessness began. Later that night he miraculously saw the drawing so vividly in Moira's bathroom.

"Yes! Of course!" he murmured and without hesitation he took the cell from the nightstand and cradled it in his hand. He wanted to do the same thing Jim did with his old one. Toss it against the wall. Instead, he dialed Moira and apologized for the late hour.

"It's okay, Tom. I miss you so much! I wish…"

"Honey," he quickly said not to misrepresent the reason of his call for he felt in Moira's voice the initiation of meowing as a cat in heat. "I must ask you a few important questions and please…never mind! Is it too late if I drop in? I'll feel more at ease to talk to you in person instead of…"

"Of course, you know that!"

As Tom stepped in, Moira with evident disappointment faced the fact that the call was strictly a business's call. But just the same she hugged him and kissed him.

"Would you like a glass of wine?"

"No thanks. This call is official not social…"

"Your job is more important to you than pleasure," she said with a faint smile. "Some day you may regret that I've cared…for you…you know?"

"Regrets! I have plenty! I'm sorry! But in the state of mind that I find myself at this point in time I'm of no use to anybody. You would regret it too if I would let the weakness of the flesh take advantage of an unstable feeling. Perhaps if I weren't a betrothed spouse to Maria whom I love, things would turn out to our benefit!" he said without conviction.

His explanations were put together well and fair, however far from being in synch with women's conjectures; men were weak and easy prey. It's only a matter of time. He'll be her lover!

"Okay, so? Am I still a suspect?" she asked.

"You're clear, I told you so. You never have to worry. But I need to ask you some simple questions and you must, I mean, must, be clear and specific. No maybes! No hesitations no matter what!"

"Okay I'm ready!" She answered calmly, still hoping to have him for the night at the end of all the questions.

"That artwork in the bathroom, you know, the one with seven arrows, where did you buy it."

"I didn't buy it. Joni, my sister, gave it to me."

"Any special reason why?"

"No! Not really! I made waves about it every time I visited her that she finally gave in and gave it to me.

"How old is she? Does she look like you? I did not meet her yet."

"How could she? She's not my biological sister! My parents adopted her...why? Why are you so interested in her? Stay away from her," she answered in a quirky attack of jealousy.

Tom smiled.

"Joni's a real beauty, a model," she continued calmly now. "She could have been a supermodel if she wasn't so crazy! She's very difficult..."

"Has she ever been married, kids, you know the whole nine yards..."

"Are you serious? She's of the opinion, why have only one man when one can have them all..."

"You do have the same option!" he wanted to say. Instead he continued to ask questions.

"Do you visit Joni often? Does she visit you often?"

"Neither!"

"You two get along well?"

"Sort of. I tolerate her a lot. So did my parents. She's a rebel!"

"Okay! The day of the assassination of the Minister you were with her all day long, correct? You two did things together? My detectives informed me that she had testified in your favor. She said you were staying at her house for three days because you were having all sorts of feuds with the Minister…"

"Why? Why are you asking me all these things?"

"Moira, you're starting with me. You'd promised me you would answer my questions. I'm not incriminating her, and definitely not you. I need as much information as I can get for my report. I don't have an easy job. The whole family has to go on file. Your parents would as well if they were alive."

"I'm sorry. I'm so confused I wish it were all over already."

"But it's not!"

Moira took a moment to recollect. Tears appeared in her eyes and between languishment and astonishment she declared her love for him in a confused but sincere rigmarole of love words. Sobbing she took his hands in hers and held them tight.

She waited for his response.

And if one taught that the investigations in comparison with the sudden declaration of love gave him discomfort, one taught wrong. Moira's was a pleasurable discomfort; a feverish desire. Suddenly, as he looked at her his whole body emanated warmth like never before. Every pore of his skin wanted her, desired her. He wanted the fusion of lust to quench the asphyxiating fire that brooded under. He wanted to melt into that fusion. He wanted to captivate her. Totally belong to her, mesmerize her, to be mesmerized by her.

Lost in oblivion behind the locked gates of an Imaginary Love Kingdom.

He felt dizzy and in his eyes sparkled an intense feeling he never felt before or maybe a forgotten feeling.

"Moira, Moira, what am I going to do with you? You make my job more difficult…"

"I'm so sorry," she blurted out crying now out loud while she put her head on his chest.

He held her closer for a few minutes. He fought the thought of having her right then and there. Instead he gently pushed her away from his body, took her face between his palms and kissed her forehead. Then he murmured.

"If I have upset you, perhaps I can come back tomorrow and finish the questions…"

"No! I'm good. Go ahead!"

"Did Joni ever leave you alone the day of the assassinations? Was she with you?" he continued taking a deep breath.

"No! She went shopping, so she said."

"Did she buy anything? Did she show you anything? You know how girls are, they like to show each other bargains."

"No!"

"How long was she gone?"

"All day!"

"All day long? You're certain?"

"Yes! I'm sure!" she mumbled.

Tom decided she had answered enough. However, speculations were all he had. Joni not being home and the art piece with the arrows were all suppositions! He must come with some hard facts! It was two o'clock in the morning when he left Moira miserably inamorata. No! Not in love! Perhaps she was infatuated. But he saw it in her eyes and the eyes tell us all. She looked at him with love in her eyes.

The next day Tom spent the entire afternoon trying to convince the prosecutor that they had a case. The chief and the captain, with doubts or without doubts, were on his side this time.

"Facts! Tom you've got to come up with hard facts not ideology?" the prosecutor told him.

"The search warrant to legally enter Joni's house will possibly give us what we're looking for." The captain cut in, in Tom's favor. Even the chief put in a few supporting words.

Finally, before closing hours that day and after hours and hours of spec-ulations, qualifications disqualified by the DA, argumentations about right and wrong within the framework of the law, which had exhausted all of the forceful resources of the lieutenant's proving points, the search warrant was finally approved.

Slapping the papers in Tom's hand the district attorney admonished, "If these investigations are not substantiated by hard facts I'm not bringing this case to court. I refuse to have a fucked up judge throw the fucking gavel on my face and kick me out of his court! Is that clear?" Thus he stormed out of sight.

This time with the chief's permission, Tom recruited all the Uniforms necessary to ransack Joni's house. Four days it took them to dislodge every suspicious piece out of every room. Moreover, they attacked the attic in search of evidences with the same frenzy hungry wolfs assault a log cabin hunting for food. They took all kinds of wigs: highlighted, black, flaming red, all in the latest styles, hunting boots and safari's outfits. Bows and arrows were also found in the attic.

Tom quickly saw her in his inner eyes as an Amazon.

However, the seven murderous arrows that impaled the guru matched none of the ones she owned. Not one that matched the fitting on the bows.

Two weeks later, just about when all that could have failed seemed to fail, Dan, with the coroner on his side, walked straight into Tom's office without knocking; sure of himself this time. So sure, he omitted his usual classic touch of hesitation before entering.

St.Thomas was sitting on his chair in the peak of doubts even though some leads about Joni's eccentric lifestyle and her sinister bent were clear. Especially incriminating was a love note that Moira found inside the frame of the arrows' picture about her ongoing affair with the Minister. More-over in Tom's favor was the fact that Joni could not produce a sound alibi of where she was during the assassinations' hours to confront and support the testimony of her innocence. Yet Tom sat immersed in profound doubts, playing with his cup of coffee and puffing on a cigarette. It seemed to be the only thing, it seemed, that alleviated the pain of his insecurity, a pain that corroded his bile.

"Come in," he just murmured to both Dan and the coroner although they were already approaching him.

"I have good news," the coroner happily said. However, as he stepped closer, he choked on the cigarette's whiff.

"The smoke in this room is denser than the inside of an Indian's tent!" Then amid coughing he reprimanded him. "You should not smoke here, you know! It's unlawful to smoke inside the building! And unhealthy!"

Tom just looked at him with half closed eyes over the rim of his glasses. The unspoken words of his disdain could be read on his face.

"The hell with you!"

On the ballot he voted against smoking prohibition. A fucking prohibition law, like the fucking twenties!

"We have two samples of hair," the coroner continued ignoring Tom's unspoken words, "One red, a tiny piece of shit that drove me crazy, attached on the spear of one of the arrows and one blonde found on the prosthetic arm. Both hairs matched Joni's wigs."

"You're kidding? Tell me you're kidding." Tom said, jumping up his chair while from his hand a jumping cup of coffee found its way down to the desk. The entire contents splashed everywhere with all the well-known consequences, not omitting the scorching of his hand.

Dan and the coroner's first reaction, as in a sudden fall of something that falls, was laughter. Secondly, as in almost every case, a realization then that, that that falls might have caused damages or injury takes place. In a case where that that fell was a person, or that that fell fell upon a person's head or in Tom's case, hand, to replace laughter with worries and concern, it is but a human character. And since the hot coffee scalded Tom's hand, the coroner's face showed concern.

Dan also showed concern and quickly ran for ice. As he was applying the ice on the scalded hand, which showed very little redness, he murmured to the coroner as if Tom wasn't there, "If you're worrying about fetching him another cup of coffee, don't bother! He never drinks it."

"He doesn't?"

"No!

"Why does he always have a cup around him? He's feeding his idiosyncrasies!" The postmortem examiner quickly analyzed.

"Beats me!" beats everybody! Dan laughed now.

"Dan, and you too Mike, Get serious! Goddamned!"

CHAPTER 18

▼

A little sense of humor was what they needed and the spilled coffee provided it. At that point all the evidence found indicated Joni as a prime suspect. However, Tom didn't seem quite ready to rush for an arrest. Other things ran through his head. The disturbing thoughts that Joni was Peter Dubois's copycat brooded over him. Furthermore, the disturbing factor that she'd followed his techniques to the smallest details, to a near science, one might say, augmented Tom's appetite to go after both of them. However, the unsettling consideration that the two characters could have been accomplices to both sets of crimes was also Tom's devil den. That abominable voice that Moira was capable to capture is the voice of Dubois, hiding somewhere in Florida, for Florida is the *Refugium peccatoris* of the land! The investigations were also proving the sinister bend to be identical. Peter and Joni abducted the victims towards illicit and perverted sexual activities, not to mention illicit drugs.

The similarity of the cases was getting disturbingly close. The most alert detectives could end up in a maze of nothingness for speculations abounded. However, Tom remained firm in his decision to follow both leads. But then again, Joni's personal style threw him off and the connection between her and Peter didn't seem right. The local victims were rich and of religious orientation whereas in Alabama they were just filthy rich commoners. That spoke clearly of a personal style. And Joni had plenty of that.

Putting it all together, Tom drew the conclusion that the ex-priest was her first and quickest victim.

Following his gut instinct and with Jim at his side, they retraced Joni's phone call to three different cab companies that delivered her and picked her up that same day on three undisclosed locations near the victims' residences.

Although he was expecting her, the ex-priest did not respond to her insistent knocking. Nevertheless, she dialed the code to open the door. She quickly drifted to where the electrical prosthetic arm was hiding, took it, and softly walked to his bedroom. Comatose under the influence of alcohol and drugs, he barely opened his eyes to the rustling of her gait closing near. "What are you doing?" he mumbled. She hurled a disdained glance at him then she pushed the open prosthetic hand around his neck. Fiercely she closed it and suffocated him.

Zip! Like a vise, zip, she sent him to hell.

She picked up the briefcase full of money and steadfastly left. She walked a block or two away from the house and called a cab. The taxi driver delivered her to a coffee shop. She ordered a cheesecake and a diet soda, gobbled the cake and drank the soda. Immediately after, like an executive from a Corporate Headquarter running late for a meeting, she walked two blocks away from the coffee shop to catch another cab that drove her near the house of the second victim, the rabbi.

Once again like an executive of a Corporate Headquarter drifting to a meeting she got to the third victim, the Minister, but a few minutes late.

The ex-priest was an electrical freak. Paul had already informed Tom. Moreover Moira, among other things, had testified that Joni was an electrical engineer, although she never worked a day in her life.

Joni's connection with the Minister had nothing to do with electricity. Lust concerned him. Money interested her.

As far as lust goes it was proven later on that the sex connection between the Minister and Joni was not an unsubstantiated assumption. As it turns out a stain of dry sperm was found on the collar of one of Joni's blouse, which had miraculously spilled and, for Tom's sake, landed there.

Moira's baseball bat, forgotten since a teenager in the attic, was the dreadful weapon of that crime. She cleaned it thoroughly and before the arrival of the last cab, a mile up from the victim's house, she threw it in a nearby lake. Then she had another taxi driver deliver her to the main entrance of the Boynton Beach Mall. With one briefcase in one hand and two in the other, she stopped at the food court and ordered an ice cream. While adrift for a few minutes near the main entrance, she was suddenly pushed by a mysterious surge. She drifted to the parking lot to fetch her Mercedes.

They voluntarily paid to meet their own death! And that interfered with the enormous amount of evidence, a lot of which however, was of circumstantial nature.

As far as the rabbi's assassination, Joni came totally clear. The dagger that had pierced the rabbi's chest many times was never found. Without a murder weapon, the DA refused to take that account to court. However, Tom didn't care much about the DA's decision. The other two old cases and the guru's were enough for indictment. And, of course, he smiled within himself thinking of the media. He was sure that if the case reached CNN, on a debate on Larry King Live, Nancy Grace would render tit for tat to the superstar lawyers.

Unlike Dubois, who stopped at the third victim, greed took over Joni and she went for the fourth; the guru whom she selected to transfix with arrows, indeed a noble death of martyrdom.

Once again, proof of Joni being the serial killer surfaced according to Gianni. The rabbi, Joni and Andrea his wife, were often engaged in a man-age-a-trois. Although screaming of innocence for any of the killings, Andrea spilled her guts to Gianni about what was going on behind closed doors in the rabbi's home. It wasn't easy for Andrea to admit it. Although hostile at first, under pressure from the young detective's accusation of complicity in the murder cases, she gave up and told him that her and Joni going down on each other gave the rabbi the necessary libido to alleviate the trauma of his erectile dysfunction.

CHAPTER 19

▼

Tom summoned his underlings to his office. He gave Loren a day off without explaining the reasons. Gianni and Phil would go to Mobile, Alabama. Tom had arranged meeting with the local sheriff. Together, step-by-step they would follow the tracks and the itinerary of Dubois's arrest and escape to the last minute detail. The previous mass of information that the lieutenant had received from Mobile was confusing and contradictory.

"Make sure to collect Dubois's photographs shot during the Mobile's police investigation. Find out the exact details about the escape! And how was it at all possible!"

He wanted his own men to go over as if it were a new crime. Interrogate people involved, presumed witness, victims' friends and enemies. The more information the better. Get tips from whoever is eager to give them. Get any information concerning that man that was not specifically laid out. And not just around Mobile but also in adjacent towns. He so badly wanted to put his hands on Dubois. However, at the same time he wanted to tie down Joni's evidences and put them in a substantial order.

Book Joni and Dubois at approximately the same time. Strike two birds with the same stone, as the popular Italian saying reminded him.

After giving his orders to Gianni and Phil, Tom sunk into deep thoughts; or perhaps he sunk into deep silence. He lit a cigarette, looked at the cup of coffee in front of him and drew it to his lips for his first sip ever.

The confused look on the detectives' faces that witnessed the event, snapped Tom out.

"Don't let it go to your head! It's fucking nasty anyhow!" he said with a chuckle.

He nodded his head and continued, "Jim, you and I, will lock each other in your crazy room till we come up with answers. As of tomorrow, say goodbye to your family. We're not going to come out until we have all the facts."

"I have a date tomorrow! I haven't seen a woman in six months..."

"She'll love you more when she finds out that your computer's ability and determination was the key to booking the killers," he just stated.

As for Dan, Tom looked at him, smiled a sad smile and then said, "You...I need you here...I...I wouldn't have known how to start my career without your support...I want you to know that no matter what this investigation...I mean whether we succeed or not! I owe you so much..." And he said it without regards to the others for it was customary of him to praise them randomly and individually and in front of others when the time rose.

At that point, Dan blushed like a shy straight A's student being praised in front of an audience for his honorable effort. He murmured a few words and blushed some more. He unawarely lifted his huge hand to his face and eclipsed that one side as to subside the upcoming heat. Then he mumbled again.

They all smiled under their noses for they knew Dan never did too well receiving unexpected praise or compliments. It must have been an effort for his blood to travel so fast and so high, especially considering his face being at the top of the 6'4 of his height. "A mountain for god's sake!" Tom thought.

He dismissed them. "Let's call it a day," he said as he was getting up. "Make sure you get a good night sleep for your nights to come might very well be sleepless."

Fine and dandy but his day was just about to begin for a bigger task was awaiting him. He had to call Maria. Placing a simple call to Maria was no longer simple. Maria had started a sequence of complaints. And Tom had

ignored them up to then. But now, after analyzing the situation, he admitted one cannot ignore loved ones. He had sporadically spoken to her but a
few times. Even worse than that he had only seen her but a few times since
the investigations began. Lets just say that those 11 months had adversely
affected their relationship. It had reached its most tense moments ever.

The easy going Lt. St. Thomas, the pleasant although tough at times Lt.
St. Thomas, had become irascible, irate, and a nervous wreck. Signs of
fatigue already showed their nasty affects. He collapsed many times into a
sudden deep sleep on his chair skipping meals while the lit cigarette wasted
away on the ashtray. Stressed out and full of doubts and fear, he studied
every aspect of interrogations and summoned more people to personally
interrogate them. The accumulated hours of work, mostly not allowed by
his superiors and or by nature's endurance, used up all his mental and
physical vital forces. However, as he dismissed everyone after the assign-
ments, he thought of Maria. He needed her. She represented the soft pillow upon which he could rest his mind and body.

Then, as of pragmatic, he took the cell in his hand and rolled it over
and over trying to block his mind away from doubts, fears, tiredness and
emotions.

Then, instinctively, Tom dialed Maria's number.

Perhaps he could humor her a bit and as she answered he quickly said,
"Are we in love?"

Of course, it backfired on him.

"Love?" she shouted. "I have no love. I have no boyfriend, I have no
husband!" And she cried out loud for an undetermined length of time.

Tom waited patiently until her crying subsided a bit then without even
thinking of the consequences, he just said, "I'm specifically calling you to
ask you to marry me."

The long silence on the other line made him nervous. Thus he uttered.
"Did you hear me? I'm asking you to marry me!"

"I've heard you. I was catching my breath."

"As soon as this ordeal is over we'll arrange our wedding...are you
there?"

"Yes!"

"That's all you have to say...I thought..."

"You don't have to marry me just because I want..."

"Maria for God' sake. I want to marry you because I love you. I want a flock of children, and I want my children with you and you only...do you hear me?"

Maria heard him but was too busy sobbing to answer him fast enough.

"Is it possible that this woman is going to drive me crazy? Isn't that what she wanted all along? But do I really want to settle down? Am I really ready to settle down? Ready to have children?"

At forty-five he asked himself if he was ready to father children?

On his way to the Yacht Club, after stopping for Chinese food to take out and running to the liquor store for a couple of bottles of wine, he murmured, "I'm forty-five, I'm fucking forty-five what am I waiting for?"

They spent a quiet night together. After dinner they sat closely and cozily while watching TV. A movie was already in progress. Minutes later, he quickly stretched on the couch and rested his head on her lap. Then he threw a melancholic glance at her and slumbered in!

At seven A.M. he walked into his office. Dan quickly followed him to hand him a note from Danny the FBI fella.

-Hey pal! Sorry I had to leave. In f... Washington, there is a talk about a long war with f... Iraq. There is need of manpower. You don't need me here! My boss is still disappointed with me for failing to convince you to join us. He calls our encounter mission impossible! Uncle Sam is saving money on you but it sure is missing a top of the line guy in its division. No use calling me, my new number is a code for now. What can I tell you? Strictly business! As soon as this ordeal is over I'll contact you, if I don't end up six feet under the sand of the desert. I've pleaded with my boss and convinced him not to send anybody to substitute me...that you work better when you work alone. I lied...I know you don't believe in lies. A white little lie won't hurt! Hey I'm your pal, no? I'm confident you're closing your investigation with a flying flag. Paula Zahn is anxious to meet you so you can talk about your greatness...AH>>>ah>>>ah>>>

God speed! Danny

Tom turned the letter over a few times, smiled softly and murmured in Italian, "*In bocca al lupo, amico*...I hope you stay away from danger!"

Dan looked at him in wonder. What was his boss all about? He didn't know the contents of the letter but he could swear Tom's eyes were at the verge of tears.

Tom raised his glary eyes halfway above his glasses at him. Then quickly to hide his emotion, he strongly said, "I'd like to know where the fuck everybody is?"

"Phil and Gianni left at five o'clock this morning heading for Mobile. I'm here as you've wished," he smiled. Then to cheer him up, he continued, "Jim has been masturbating the computer since six. That's it! Oh, Loren is making coffee...She refused to take a day off. Do you want a cup?"

"Fuck the coffee! Let's motivate!"

The humor was achieved. They both laughed.

CHAPTER 20

▼

The captain and the chief were now anxious to book Joni after going over the report full of overwhelming evidence. Although half of it was of circumstantial nature, at last they felt they had a case. Even the prosecutor, wiping out his moments of negativity, was willing to take a risk and bring the case to court. But to everybody's astonishment, Tom steered clear of any rush.

"Things are missing! We're not yet in synch! We do not want to make a mistake. We must be sure! The paperwork is half done! We have to organize and reorganize things!"

In his mind Peter Dubois was constantly seizing him into frenzy. Running out of excuses, he was afraid that time wouldn't allow him to book Joni and Dubois at the same time. He wanted both the original and the copy brought in at approximately the same time. He was sure, at least now, that Joni was Dubois' copycat but Peter was yet not at hand. He was invisible.

"Invisible, he repeated over and over."

Paul flashed in his mind. He was determined to see and check his eyes. No! Paul is a loser, full of air and full of money. Criminal? Impossible! He is no criminal!

Waiting to make a decision, he spent his time at Jim's wire-room. He speculated about the evidence without substantiality coming to the surface of things. Furthermore, his closeness frustrated and agitated Jim to no end and he made no secret about.

He momentarily returned to his office. He shuffled a bunch of papers laid upon his desk and back he went to the wire-room or arsenal of electric wires. Quietly and anxiously he stood a decent distance from Jim. Paul flashed again and again in his head.

"Stop everything! We must find a new approach! I want the names of unlicensed doctors...dermatologists, plastic surgeons..."

"What town?"

"The county!"

"The county?"

"Yes! The fucking county! The peninsula! The whole fucking peninsula..."

He furiously stepped out. In an effort to appear calm to Loren he lowered his speed as he walked by her desk. In vain, Loren was not in sight.

He then slowly returned to his office and lit a cigarette at the door. When he reached his desk, he stood looking at the amount of papers he had previously browsed, laid in messy heaps. He took a meaningless and disinterested look at them.

Meanwhile he talked to himself. Monomania, he called it. "My living hell, my delirium tremens. Little do I know about Loren and Paul's relationship? Did she love him? Did he love her? No! Paul couldn't love anybody! Perhaps the possibility of being a killer...Paul? It's Paul's life style that bothered me. Free of worries and a life secured by money, lots of money. Moreover, if Paul were a killer why did he hang around the station talking to Loren with an air of know-it-all? Displaying vibes of well being mixed with an acquired childish attitude as that of a rich spoiled brat. Is it the noblesse oblige aura, the wealth, that rich spoiled-brat-attitude that appalls me?"

Loren, thank God, stepped in, thus interrupting his nonsensical self-mumbling. Cheerfully she walked in with a disposition to converse. He looked at her and remembered the day off. However he pointed his index at the chair across the desk.

As she sat he said, "Am I wrong in assuming...didn't I give you...I thought I gave you a day off..."

"Insubordination! I think it's called. I'm needed here today more than ever!" she said impertinently.

"Okay, since it was your choice and since I see that you're in a chatting mood, answer a few questions for me," he said with his eyes, drooping from over the rims of his glasses and looking into hers.

"Shoot!" she still cheerfully said.

"But if for whatever reason you don't feel up to...this is very difficult for both of us."

The cheerfulness and happy disposition suddenly turned into worries. She murmured, "Please Tom don't scare the living lights out of me! I've chosen to be here today. That doesn't mean you have to scare me!"

"Didn't mean to! I need Paul's most recent photos..."

"Oh my God..."

"...Without his glasses," he continued ignoring the interruption. "Do you really love this guy?" he suddenly blotted out.

"No, not really!" she responded after a moment of hesitation. Then she put him at ease when she continued sure of herself. "Besides, money or no money, I'm getting sick and tired of all this invisibility! I need a more stable man in my life. I'm getting old. I want a family. I want kids!"

Thus he caught the occasion to clearly and freely speak to her without the usual preamble. "We have reason to believe that Paul...Paul might just about be our murder suspect!"

"Oh My God," she shouted putting her face in the palm of her hands. Then tears came out of her eyes and sobbing she murmured as if talking to herself, "I...All this time...I was living in danger and didn't even know it!"

"Nay, you were not!"

"Why not! If he turns out to be the killer..."

"...Not on your salary," he said forcing a smile upon himself. "He is, assuming we're right, not the usual type. Not at all one of those blood-thirsty killer that kills for the heck of killing. He's a thief killer, a sophisticated killer. He only kills for millions of dollars, otherwise he doesn't bother. You and I are not on his list!" He forced himself to smile again.

She remembered having taken a surprise photo or two of Paul without glasses. She also remembered that Paul seized into frenzy for her audacity, scaring the hell out of her. Everything was coming clear to her again. Soon after, Paul amply apologized to her but kept a scornful yet satanic grin that caused her a sudden fear.

That scary scene, together with his fixation of invisibility, his secrets, the fact that he lived like a gipsy, no established residence, no contact with any family's members, no friends, no signs of desire to commitment of any kind, all gave her a bad taste in her mouth that gradually built hostility.

CHAPTER 21

▼

The mere fact that Tom presented Paul to Loren as a presumed suspect increased her hostility towards her lover ten-fold.

And for a while now Tom felt the vibes that Loren was experiencing frustration and change of moods about her relation. In fact, lately she had shown plenty of swings. Thus Tom's questions and the request of the lover's photo without sunglasses came at the right time. Although reluctant at first, but more so for fear of Paul than the will to cooperate, she agreed to produce Paul's photos. However, when Tom pushed a little more and asked her to produce a tape with Paul's voice to compare it with that of Peter's, she went into hysterics.

She was his only hope. He needed to compare the two men's voice. After Moira had acknowledged that the last tape she'd listened was Peter Dubois's voice, Tom felt the similarity in Paul's diction. But then again sometimes he didn't. He needed Paul's taped voice. If Paul's voice in a tape matched that of Peter, then that voice belonged to the same person. He'll book Paul as prime suspect as being Dubois incarnated. Name, new face, camouflaged voice, and new residence...Florida! Here, under the name of Paul Invisible, lives busily squandering nine million dollars.

However, to look at Loren so hysterically frightened, Tom made the quick decision, however disappointed, to put it off and postpone it all for later days. She needed serious time to get over the shock.

He walked her to the door with his arm around her shoulder. Then he said, "Don't worry. You don't have to do anything if you are not emotionally up for it!" while his hand gently caressed one side of her face.

Just as she left, Jim walked in.

"I have the profile of four unlicensed doctors. However, to save you time and to suit my criteria I had it narrowed to one. Dr. Jones under a new name, of course!

"So? Give me the new name!"

"Dr. Smith! He lives in Miami, Little Havana. I have his address and all. According to my investigation it seems that the dean of BR Community Hospital, with the help of three other doctors, accused him of illegally performing surgery on a young boy. The medical term escapes me at the moment but I have it in the profile. The boy survived after complications of all sorts. Five years ago there was a lot of commotion about Dr. Jones' case!"

"Okay! Give me the papers I'll go over them now!"

A few days later, Phil and Gianni had come back from Mobile with boxes filled with old and new information. Tom spent days reading it all. He was ready! This was the booking time! However, he needed and wanted to meet with Doctor Smith first. He needed to sat the record straight. It was a must!

Tom drove full speed to Miami. It took him two hours before finding a benefactor who knew exactly where Dr. Smith could be found, since the knocks at the door produced no results.

"If you're looking for Doc he's not home…" A voice came from behind him.

"Yeah! I'm looking for Doctor Smith! So where is he?" Tom asked as he turned around to face the boy that had spoken behind his back.

"Who needs him?"

"I need to talk to him. It's an emergency…"

"…Emergency my ass!"

"Okay, cut the shit, it's important that I see him."

"He practically lives at the beach, South Beach, between 13th Street and 15th Street…" said the boy who appeared to be a loafer.

"Of course with some little token, you'll come with me and show me the exact location," Tom said seriously.

"Of course! You know we all have to make a living. You know? But to tell you the truth, I'm not so crazy about your attitude," he said in a philosophical tone.

"I'm in tears, have pity on me! How much?"

"One hundred bucks!"

"Hey, hey, take it easy, I'm a poor man…"

"Poor man my ass, lieutenant!"

"How do you know I'm a lieutenant?"

"The smell!"

"I took a shower this morning," Tom said with a smile.

"Nevertheless, I smelled you just the same…" he answered nonchalantly.

"Get in the car José!"

"Jose'? How do you…

"The smell!" Tom burst laughing. "Okay, let's go! You'll take the bus back. This kind of money could buy you a ticket back to Cuba to visit your mamasita." Thus he handed him the bill.

José took it. He flagged it over his eyes, he made a few facial assumptions and as if he were a banker, valued it not to be a counterfeit, and then pocketed it.

On the way to the renowned South Beach, José talked continuously yet Tom hardly followed his dialogue. However, he couldn't help smiling here and there for José's tongue hitting his teeth in every said word reminded him of the Cuban accent Al Pacino mimicked so well in ScarFace.

"Hey lieutenant, make a right here. Shit, you passed it!"

Tom backed up and took 13th Street. Then he skillfully maneuvered the car into the first available space.

"Cool!" the kid proffered full of admiration. "Cool man! That's cool!"

"Never mind! Let's go!" he said quickly getting out of the car.

"Hey, aren't you going to put money in the meter?"

"Evidently you don't think you cost me enough. Come on let's go. He'd better be here or I'll take my money back."

They crossed the street and walked towards the sea.

"Wait!" José suddenly said and halted as he spotted Doctor Smith. "I don't want him to see me. That one, the one sitting all alone."

"The one with the hat on?"

"Yeah!" I must run!"

Tom grabbed him strongly by the arm causing him to scream.

"If you've led me wrong I'll find you. Be sure of that!"

"Let go of me you're hurting me! That's him, man! Let go of me!"

CHAPTER 22

▼

Tom stood a few yards in back of Dr. Smith. And then he walked around to get in front of him. He saluted him.

Dr. Smith didn't deign to raise his eyes.

"Doctor Smith, I was wondering if I could have a few words with you," he said and he showed him his badge.

"Verily whoever you are, you have nothing to say that would interest me," the doctor said still keeping his eyes down.

"Perhaps half a million dollars would change your mind. I want a change of looks. I no longer like my Italian Provincial face!"

Dr. Smith slowly raised his eyes towards Tom. He threw him a hateful glance and then turned his head the other way. Tom anticipated his move and pivoted on his heels to face him again.

"Doctor! It's not my intention to make it difficult for you. However, you are leaving me no choice. If the tenor of your manners remains the same I'll take strong aggressive measures. We can either talk calmly now and without reluctance to avoid taking authority's enforcement thus allowing me precautionary exercise…meaning I'll summon you up with all due regards of the law to appear at BBPD headquarter in the Palm Beaches. My Captain is a nasty son of a bitch…a real bastard…since birth!"

"What is it that you want from me?"

"I'm not after you! I couldn't give a fuck how many millions of dollars you've pocketed and how many works of arts you've performed on people's faces. I'm only interested in one person, a certain Peter Dubois. Come clear and I clear you! In my lingo I'll cut you a deal. Any other way I'll nag you, hound you, trail you, harass you until you drop dead!"

"You leave me no choice?" he said already mellowing.

"No choice!"

"I was a good doctor! I'm still one of the best..."

"I've never had a doubt. I've read your court's ordeal. I sympathize with you! There is nothing you can add to your benefits...I know all about you: your nationality, where you come from, old marital status and the two nasty divorces...your PhD in medicine Cum Laude. Your superior performances in the *cutting room*."

"It was a plot! A conspiracy! The operation was a success!" They did something to the kid to delay his recovery. He survived because I took every precaution. It was an experimental procedure. Against their reluctance I followed through with it. I knew what I was doing..." he said convinced. "The surgery was a success!" he repeated a few times. "The boy was manhandled by all of the them, including nurses and orderlies. They caused the recovery's retardation. It was jealousy! They hated my guts..."

"As I said beforehand, I know! I would cut a deal for you! You'd never have to worry..."

"Yeah, never have to worry! For the rest of my life..."

"Doctor, let's cut the shit out! You're making lots of money in a clandestine way. I'll make sure you can keep on doing it undisturbed. Just like you in your profession, I am one of the best in mine! And I know exactly what I can do for you!"

Dr. Smith, although still hesitant, was already convinced. There was something about that young lieutenant that inspired trust. Something special about his clean cut face. Not handsome, but pleasant; his narrow shoulders, his wiry arms and legs, the gait of a hungry feline. But more than his physical aspect, the doctor saw the other side of the man: tenacity, moral strength, sure of himself, professionally equipped with the right intelligence and seriousness.

And to compliment it all, his brown eyes dotted with golden spots sparkled an inner depth mixed with confidence and resolve. Moreover, when they stared at you they imprinted compassion, love for the innocents and perhaps love for the guilty ones. Perhaps unknown to himself he chose that job, unworthy as it were, to share in the struggle among others of good will, to help minimize the sins of the human folly.

"What do you want to know about Peter?" he serenely asked with a twitch of the lips that shuttered a sad smile.

"All!"

And thus the doctor spoke.

"You must believe me, I knew nothing about that Mobile killing during plastic surgery. I wouldn't have…It wouldn't have mattered how much…I'm a born doctor. I believe in life not death. By pure chance three years ago, I came across the atrocious killing in Alabama on the Miami Herald during a visit to Miami's library. I became interested and read it all. I followed it step by step but I got confused about the photos in the newspapers. There was a certain resemblance but I couldn't put my fingers on it. I remembered very little about his old face. He burned the photos that I shut as preambles before every procedure. And, of course, he gave me a fictitious name…Ed Morris, I think. It's in my file. I keep all my files in a bank box. But…"

"…But?"

The doctor went into silence and then turned his eyes at Tom and just uttered, "I need a beer! Can I buy you one?"

"Sure! We can finish this conversation on the strip in one of those outside cafes."

He also needed to be quenched. His lips were so dry that he wet them with his tongue but his own saliva gave him nausea. The dog day afternoon didn't provide the breather with what the Atlantic Ocean's light breeze usually offers as a matter of fact at that particular hour of the day. Moreover, the relentless sun, without any signs of clouds in the sky, pondered over his head with its perpendicular rays. The beige linen shirt was glued with sweat against his torso and spine. His blue linen trousers changed color to a nasty unfamiliar tone.

They sat silently on a corner under the shade produced by an umbrella, both attacking their bottle of beer as if all the breweries were about to close shutters forever.

As Tom had basically emptied his bottle in a single gulp, he took a breather and asked again, "but?"

"But," the doctor said and he paused a few seconds for he also was catching up on his breathing. "But I'll never forget his eyes…"

"…His eyes?" Tom asked. "What about his eyes?"

"His eyes spit fire, horror, hate in search of a prey at all times."

"If I show you recent photos of Dubois with his new face," he said thinking of the photos that Loren shot of Paul without dark glasses, "would you be able to qualify those eyes as of then?"

"Yes! Of course! I told you. I would recognize them among thousands! Are you taping this conversation?" The doctor suddenly asked him.

"Why waste time on stupidity when in a court of law it doesn't mean a damned thing?"

CHAPTER 23

▼

One must know that Lieutenant St. Thomas was born unconventional, as he himself liked to say. He never carried a gun. Not on a daily basis like all the other members of the law enforcement agencies. Was he a sharp-shooter just the same? By all means! One of the best! But he felt there was a bit of ostentation, a tinge of chauvinism to carry a gun during office's hours; on a shopping spree for clothes or go after what he called *ladri di galline* (chicken coup's thief). However, when it was a killer that he was dealing with, besides carrying the gun he also wore a bulletproof vest.

Time for the show down drew closer. Overwhelming evidence showed Joni to be the killer of the three religious men in Florida. He also fingered Paul as Dubois's *incarnito* and as the killer of the Alabama's men. Loren was capable of producing Paul's photos without the dark glasses and tapes of his voice. Scrupulously checked, both the eyes on the photos and the taped voice were, indeed, the same as those of Peter Dubois's. All the pieces fit.

Mr. Paul Invisible was indeed Peter Dubois!

Lieutenant St. Thomas no longer felt any doubt. He had never been so ready or so sure of himself. After taking into consideration that Paul and Joni could be accomplices on the two sets of terrible crimes, Tom made the decision, right there and then, to book them both.

To Gianni and Phil he just said, "Go read Joni her rights!"

Dan stayed with Tom to adjust his vest and make sure the cartridge case was loaded. He took precautions to fill the pockets of his jacket with extra bullets. Then he looked deeply at him.

"Perhaps I should watch over your shoulders?"

Tom did not answer. And Dan just shook his head.

It had become a personal matter.

Tom had to capture Paul by himself. He wanted to know the why; a full confession! To better understand people perhaps? What makes a killer? And how does one go over the edge?

On the way to arrest and/or capture Paul, Tom appeared calm while hiding trains of thoughts intermingled, twisted, twined towards confusion. Indeed a confused finale. Innocent? Guilty? Perhaps both! Both? How can it be both? One is either innocent or guilty! Period. And in all that confusion, he thought of his job. Why? What turned him on? Why did he choose that kind of work? Then the answer came rather easily. Even as a young adult he thought some day he would become an investigator. He clearly couldn't remember but he did remember that he badly wanted to be a cop, an investigator, and especially an undercover cop. Perhaps the power behind it! After college, after the nuisance of many shortcomings about reality and facts of life with seriousness and tenacity, he went for it. He wanted to be somebody. He wanted to be a cop and thus climbed the stairs of rank, quickly and honorably.

When Tom left for the hunting, Jim was still in his wired-room, obsessed, working his last details on Dubois.

"Fuck!" he murmured. "A half brother! Where does this come from? The motherfucker has a half brother. So Paul is not Peter! Peter could be the killer...Paul perhaps has nothing to do with all this. Tom went to arrest the wrong man! Or perhaps they were together...all was falling into place...on the Alabama's serial assassinations!"

He printed the information and stormed out of the door, bouncing inside his clothes like a loose spring dropped from above, leaping towards the office to see Tom.

"What is it? He's gone! He left an hour ago. Where have you been?" Dan said with half a smile. The excitement that lived inside that kid's nervous system always humored him.

But Jim didn't smile. Oh no! When Jim pursued something he didn't come up for air till he tracked it down bits by bits, while his nervous system vibrated like the strings of a violin hitting new cords.

"Alone? You fuck! Let him go alone…always thought tall men were fucking stupid…a half brother, can't you understand, a half brother…"

"Calm down! What the fuck are you talking about?"

"Fucking bunch of yellowbellies. Where are the other two assholes? Those two fucking losers…he doesn't carry a gun and you all let him go to a fucking criminal as if he was going to church."

It took awhile for Jim to calm down and a longer while for Dan to understand what that nonsense was all about.

"Jesus! God almighty!" It quickly dawned on him, "a half brother?"

That meant Tom was perhaps chasing the wrong one. Or perhaps, both brothers were hunting for Tom.

"Change of plans! Forget Joni," Dan quickly radioed Gianni and Phil. "Meet Jim and I at Lake Worth Municipal Casino's parking lot. I'll call back from my car and explain it all. Start moving! Now! And no sirens!" he basically shouted in full command which surprised Jim but mostly himself.

They arrived at the parking lot within minutes of one another. Dan and Jim spread apart as total strangers; likewise did Gianni and Phil. Independently, they scouted the area in every direction, trying to look as inconspicuous as possible and not to raise any suspicion. They reunited at the steps that led to the Pier. No sign of Tom or Paul! And to radio Tom was not the most intelligent action to take. But Jim was restless. He rolled his cell in his hand. He then passed it to the other hand and cradled it.

"If you thinking of calling, don't. It could be intercepted by Paul and expose Tom," Dan said with a tone of command throwing a menacing look at his restless partner.

Tom already had Paul within his gun's range in an undisclosed place. Finally, he opened the elements of his suspicion in every detail and urged Paul to admit it all.

"You're crazy Lieutenant St. Thomas," Paul addressed him formally with a faint smile that showed neither the truth or a lie!

"Yeah! I am! But you're a killer even worse, a serial killer and as you've just reminded me, I am a lieutenant and in charge of reading you your rights!" And he had just started, "You have the right…"

He picked up the ringing cell and Jim screamed from the other line, "Where are you? We're looking all over…"

"Calm down, I'm fine. I'll be at the station in an hour. Stay calm, all of you!"

It was of no use. Jim boiled inside his clothes ignoring all his partners' scolding glances. He kept on talking to Tom. "I must tell you. Don't hang up the phone on me. I must tell you…Peter Dubois is Paul's half brother…"

"Brother? Half brother? Are you fucking sure?" He asked and quickly looked at Paul who just lowered his eyelids over his eyes.

"I'm positive I've just found out. I have the printout and a photo with me…"

"Where are you?"

"At the Pier! We're walking back to our cars…"

"…Our cars?" I thought I made it clear for all of you to stay away…forget about it, just meet me at the parking lot below; the smaller one north of the big on the park side, next to A1A."

Ten minutes later Tom stormed into the small parking lot with screeching tires and skidded into the middle of the other two unmarked cars. He quickly stepped out of his car and locked it leaving Paul inside. He took Jim's material in his hand. No need to read it all. The eyes on the photo were as if transplanted from Peter's socket into Paul's or vice versa. Moreover, the resemblance, even with the plastic surgery of Peter's face, clearly showed they were at least half biologically bonded.

Like Jim, Tom thought the two half brothers could have been involved in these crimes together. Clearly the cases showed different styles and different weapons. However, Tom had no time to evaluate the whole ordeal now. He had to move and move fast! Since Paul was already in his custody, Peter could have been on his way to Doctor Smith to do him in. Tom couldn't allow it.

Thus to Gianni and Phil he said, "Go finish your job. Go read Joni her rights!" To Dan and Jim he ordered, "You two, handcuff him and book him! Don't release him no matter what, even if you have to hide him from the captain and the chief. And don't allow him to place a call to a lawyer until I'm back, perhaps in two or three hours. Maybe four," he added. But a nasty thought entered his mind; maybe never! Which he quickly wiped out.

The stubbornness with which Tom wanted to capture Peter alone was not shared with his helpers but they didn't say a word. However, Jim grabbed Dan's elbow for among them he was the senior officer, as if to say, "put your foot down! Don't you see he's seized by frenzy?"

Dan pulled away from Jim's grip and in anger just said, "You must learn, my boy, to execute orders at the same fucking moment they're given! And I'm ordering you to go to handcuff that sonofabitch in Tom's car and throw him in ours!" Then turning to Tom he just murmured, "Lieutenant SanTommaso, be careful and In...In Bo..."

"...In bocca al lupo..."

"...Yeah that! Should I follow you at a safe distance? Perhaps..."

"No! It would be too dangerous for me and also for you! I'll be fine. I must go before he gets to Doctor Smith before me. I promised him nothing would ever happened to him if I could help it."

Thus he stepped into his car, ignoring Paul's plea to set him free, while Jim literally threw him in their car.

I-95 south. He blasted his siren up to the threshold of Miami. As he entered the neighborhood, he shut it and searched both sides of the street hoping to spot Al Pacino's double. Tom had been totally taken by Pacino's performance in Scarface and had watched the movie many times. Now being in the same area, same streets, same environment, he smiled for the first time that day thinking of the actor and how so powerfully he impersonated the charisma of young Cubanos and their lingo.

As he got closer to the apartment house, he parked the car. He checked his pistol, put it back in the holster, adjusted his bulletproof vest, took a deep breath and stepped out. Doubts, fear, misconceptions gave him a feverish inertia and every thought that bounced in his mind came twisted and went out even more twisted.

He rested against his car.

Threw a quick distract glance in all directions.

He looked tired, emaciated. He toiled towards his last wind. He stretched his back away from his car and sighed. What was he looking for? Tom didn't know Peter. What did he look like? Was there a resemblance between him and Paul? Peter had a new face! Perhaps, being half brothers they had the same mannerism? He needed an inspiration, but can one find a killer on inspiration only? Where was the mythical beacon of the forest that shows the lost hero or heroine the way out?

Find Peter there? In Miami? Miami is a large city! How would Peter know that he had contacted Doctor Smith and that the doctor had spilled his guts to him. But unless the doctor comes with Peter's profile and all, it is not going to help any in a court of law. And Doctor Smith had stated that although he performed his surgeries with an irreversibly revoked license, he never forgot that he was a doctor and recorded all his work. However, he'd also stated the Peter had burned his photos. The medical paperwork was in a bank box. But that's just for the doctor's benefit. Tom would get no gain from the rigmarole of medical terminology.

A silhouette playing hide and seek behind the corner of a building snapped him out. He went straight for his gun but quickly let his hand drop down along his leg. Adrift and displaying a blasé mannerism, as if a tourist, throwing an eye here and there, he wanted to appear. Then he calmly steered clear of the site and turned around.

Whoever was hiding behind the corner had fell for it.

Tom quickly made an abrupt turn on his heels, located the leaving character and followed him. At a faster pace he reached him. He put his hand on the holster without pulling the gun out and shouted, 'Freeze!'

And José froze.

"Turn around!" Tom commanded.

"Hey man, I know nothing," he said reluctantly still with his back towards Tom.

"Turn around or I'll blow your head off!" Tom commanded but still kept his gun inside the holster.

"Have you seen this man around?" he asked flushing Peter's photo as the boy slowly turned to face him.

"I know nothing I'm telling you!"

"Okay let me make it easy for you," Tom said controlling his adrenaline that was already hitting the high stage of his tolerance. "You either cooperate with the law enforcement or I'll make sure you spend the rest of your life in the scummiest can in the State of Florida. Those old criminals always welcome pretty boys like you." Then he added just in case Jose' didn't grasp the metaphor, "In other words as soon as they see you coming, they're going to arrange where and when it becomes more suitable to attend to their business…"

"No! Man!" he exclaimed with a painful look on his face as if things were already happening.

"Do you want me to be more fucking explicit?" he said putting the weight on the four-letter word.

"No, man you have nothing on me man!"

"No! But I'll find a way. In fact I'm going to tell you what I'll do. I'll have few of my men stuff your room with cocaine…and with a search warrant, thereafter, they'll rake your room upside down, find the kilos hidden under you mattress and bye-bye José."

"Hey man…"

"Let me show you the photo again. Have you?"

"Hey man…do you want to see me dead?"

"When I put my hands on him he'll have no breath left to call your name never mind come looking for you! And you'll be the hero of your neighborhood. So the sooner you'll tell me the sooner you'll be famous!"

"Hey man he's a nasty looking dude. He terrifies me…"

"Where? How? Where is he? I'm running out of time. Specify, where? Goddamned!"

"I saw them taking the bus to South Beach..."

"...Them? Doctor Smith was with company. The man in the photo...talk goddamned!"

"The way it looks the doctor is not coming back man..."

Tom suddenly ran to his car. Quickly he started the engine and speeded up to South Beach, leaving Jose' stunned in the middle of the street. José frowned at the car speeding away, and then a smile that cherished a sudden admiration rose to his lips. Thus he proffered, "That fucking lieutenant is a crazy fuck! Man...a real crazy fuck!"

St. Thomas, as he'd done with José, inadvertently passed 13th Street. He jammed on the brakes, backed up and parked at the end of the street. Then he slowly walked southbound. His gut feeling kept him looking towards the bistro where he had interrogated the doctor months before. He sensed the doctor would use his shrewdness to direct Peter to the same café and perhaps if it was vacant the same table. Thus facilitating Tom's hunting. He had promised Tom to cooperate even though his life was on the line. Peter was an assassin and Doctor Smith has suspected then and knew it now.

"I want a change of looks," Peter posing as Ed Morris, an industrial mogul, had told him.

"Mask it, that's what he wanted. Disguise it."

The Doctor's profound anger against societies, the hate towards his own kin and colleagues that brazenly confabulated against him drew him to make the wrong decision. Thus he started practicing medicine, illegally. He was disappointed at justice. Indeed, angry! Instead of protecting him, justice was allowed to revoke his license forever.

Of course, he tried to reinstate it through a judicial chain of court of appeals from which he repeatedly met denial, on many accounts.

Five years of illegally practicing medicine got him tired. He sometime dreamed he could have lived a different life. As a result, the thought of quitting was constantly on his mind; perhaps, move on to other things or to other countries. But the doctor in him always prevailed to stay hidden in Miami in scummy little two rooms.

For God's sake! Life and saving lives was the very reason he'd chosen medicine. Not fame, not money, but life! He was one of those rare and dedicated species that helped poor people. He never put money ahead of his duty; the duty towards his patients. He took desperate cases under his care for small compensation and many times assisted, pro bono, with drugs included, penniless uninsured patients. He wanted to be an innovator, a scholar, and not a moonlighting legal-drug dealer. He bargained swapping favor with pharmaceutical sales persons, a few friends indeed, that kept their silence and believed justice had done him wrong. They sympathetically tried to help him by supplying leftover samples for his most needy patients. His plastic lifting and re-lifting of faces could have allowed him to live a wealthy life. However, he anonymously sent most of his earnings to medical research while keeping just enough money to support a mere living.

He talked to Peter with calmness and conviction, making no display of any fear even though he had a rough time trying to control his churning stomach. He was well aware of his destiny, although he couldn't figure out why Peter didn't finish him in the solitude of his squalid apartment. Why drag him to South Beach, a place swarming with people, taking chances to be caught in the act? What was the purpose? However, considering Peter's insanity and history of criminality, anything was possible. And why give him rope when at the end of the rope his expiration date was already numbered?

Meanwhile at BBPD the commotion was unbearable. Dan avoided looking at Loren. Her eyes were smeared with tears.

Phil and Gianni had not yet returned with Joni and the Uniforms were restless. Scattered around the corridor, they waited for orders that did not come. The captain, sat in his office, worried stiff. He mentally inveighed against Tom, who against his better judgment had pursued Peter, a man at large and unreachable, without asking advice or help from his superiors. The Alabama killer with a new face, new name and nine million dollars to squander would definitely have chosen to live incognito in Florida, a stone fling from Mobile. However, at that point in time the captain's only worries concerned Tom's safety. He nervously waited for the chief who always in oblivion and who prolonged instead of speeding up the conference he was attending.

Jim went in and out of his wired-room silently and unbelievably calm, nodding his head. Finally, he approached Dan and again unbelievably calm, totally contrary to his springing-nervous-wreck body movements, he just said, "I have read Tom's notes about the meeting with Dr. Smith. The location where they first met, the name of the bistro even the table they sat. I know South Beach like the palm of my hand…perhaps…"

"I read it also!" Dan murmured.

"Perhaps…"

"…Yeah! We're going! Check your gun! Put your vest on! Get ready!" He commanded in full control of the circumstances, contrary to his character. And for the first time ever since the beginning of his career, he disobeyed orders.

"I'm ready!" Jim said as a matter of fact.

"Me too! Let's go!"

CHAPTER 24

▼

Tom walked slowly shaving the walls of the buildings with his shoulder. The sweat poured down from every pore of his skin. The vest made its weight feel the heat. The thermostat outside of a café marked 92 degrees F with relatively humidity, which felt like one hundred and fifty degrees on his body. He thought, 'I'll collapse before I reach them,' but he kept on going.

His guess about the spot was dead on. The doctor somehow had made sure as he selected same umbrella on the same corner. He spotted them. Also, another smart move by the doctor, whether it be coincidental or arranged, he had Peter sit on the chair that faced south while he sat across the table facing north. From that position where Tom would come looking for him, if and only if, Tom was on the right track.

However, Doctor Smith had confidence in Tom. He had the hunch since the first encounter that the lieutenant didn't come up for air in his pursue of a suspect.

And it proved right when Dr. Smith saw the figure of a man, a few blocks away, coming his way. He could swear it was Tom grazing the walls.

Suddenly, fearful of raising Peter's suspicions, he lowered his eyes to avoid the temptation to look beyond him. Instead he talked to distract him.

"The lieutenant came to me by word of mouth. It was nothing more than a simple consultation for a future nose job. But even if he'd come to investigate me I wouldn't have, assuming you've committed the crimes, giving you up. There was no gain to give you up in the situation I'm in. I'm an outlaw myself."

Of course, Peter didn't believe a word he'd said and calmly without even moving a hair he just said, "Doctor Smith, your time has come. I knew that sooner or later you would cause me problems. I should have eliminated you right after the surgery. You know…I have a heart. At any rate be thankful. You had a good life thus far."

A sarcastic hateful roar of laughter followed his saying, which made the doctor instantly drip sweat. However, calmly he stood and then with dignity murmured, "I'm ready for whatever my destiny will be. As for you, killing me is only going to cause suspicion in the investigators even more and start a chain-reaction that'll do you in."

"Cut the bullshit and let's get the fuck out of here!"

"I'm ready!"

"How much money is in the briefcase?"

"All I had! It's filled to the top with twenties and fifties. I didn't count it. Perhaps a couple hundreds! It was money ready to be sent for charity!"

"Perhaps a couple hundreds? Ready to be sent for charity?" he mimicked him. "Could have done better! And what's this charity bullshit"

"That's all I had!" The doctor just murmured.

"Come on move!"

"Please allow me to pay the bill," he said procrastinating. Indeed the man shaving the walls with his shoulder could just about be Tom. "I'm a patron here. I will feel terrible if they think I left without paying."

"Sure! It will be terrible to feel that way…from your coffin!" he said and dashed a laugh. "Sure, call the waiter!"

The doctor looked around to get the waiter's attention but mostly hoped to see Tom closing in on them. But he had lost track of him. There were no indications of the Tom's whereabouts. Instantly his stomach registered pain and gripping churns. "Perhaps," he then thought a little more confidently, "Perhaps, the cop, that lieutenant has his own weird ways. Perhaps he does have the ability to conceal himself from a killer."

No, Tom was not around in person nor in disguise. God only knows, where Tom was heading at that time. He was a detective, for God's sake, not a clairvoyant. How did it all happen so fast? Last time the doctor met with the investigator he had told him that the time to close in on Dubois was at hand. It was a week ago and hell had since broken loose in his mind. The fear that Peter would get to him, as it was a matter of fact now, before the lieutenant could arrange things for his safety, gave him sleepless nights followed by horrendous nightmares.

"I'm sure the lieutenant meant well!" he thought. "However I'm in this mess and I don't see the way out!"

He diagnosed his own coming cardiac arrest. He wished it on himself. It would be less painful and more human than having his brains blown up.

"Please," he said with a tread of voice, a shaky murmur, to a waiter that passed by their table, "please the check!"

"Yes Doc! I'll send George over!"

A few minutes later, the attending waiter showed up. He stood with his back towards Peter and said. "Doc, Mr. Rossini would have come to tell you himself, but he got tied up on the way here. At any rate, he told me to tell you "it's on the house today."

The doctor's face radiated instantly and his heart resumed a more normal beat at the moment he recognized Tom in guise of a waiter, however, for a futile moment...a futile moment indeed!

"Turn around, you, show me your face! Turn!" Shouted the criminal. Then to Tom's hesitation he sarcastically continued, "come on, lieutenant, sir! You're making me angry. Take the empty chair next to the doctor. Now!" he warned while he rattled the pistol under the table.

"What..." Tom confusedly murmured, turning to face him.

"Shutthefuckup and sit or I'll do you both in right now!" he said raising the tone of his voice still rattling the barrel of his gun against the leg of the table.

Tom sat.

In that split second, all of his tactics vanished. Contradicting feelings ran in and out of his mind.

"I'm done! Perhaps, I'll be fast enough if I jump on him and take possession of the gun." To think of doing it and to do it were two different things. He remained nailed down to his chair while his limbs stiffened. He instantly felt bloodless.

An empty shell!

CHAPTER 25

▼

An empty shell just like when at 15 years old, in Italy, a terrible ugly dude wanted to steal his brand new bike. It was just the beginning of dusk. Tommaso had mounted his bike and went for a ride at the town garden. He rolled closer to the wrought iron bench, he stopped and raised one foot from the pedal and placed on the seat to balance himself. Then he smiled as he looked at the show of lights down below in the adjacent towns. And the conflict with the burning gases of combustion shooting out of smokestacks of the newly industrial refineries. The beginning of pollution and the end of what was once beneficial clean and clear air.

He felt a rustling coming from the bushes and the sudden assault to the nostril of a horrendous body odor. He turned around and froze.

"You little shit, give me that bike!" ordered the man with lice flying around his long beard and a knife in his hand.

"It's my bike!"

"It was your bike!" he said while he pushed the bike making Tommaso flying off and hitting the ground hard. He quickly mounted the bike and pedaled on.

Tommaso felt lost. What was he going to tell his father? He wanted to scream for help and hopefully attract attention. Nobody seemed to be around…tears blinded him. He then wiped them off in anger. He got up and ran after the offender. He ran fast those days. He reached the man, and ran along the bike avoiding the kicks the thief unsuccessfully delivered.

"Give me the bike pig," he shouted, but the man cycled on. "*Figlio di puttana*, I'll kill you!"

Tommaso couldn't give up. He wanted his bike! This time he did not call the man names, he did not say a word, he just acted. He stuck his hand under the rope that acted as a belt, and pulled him off the bike. The bike spun ahead and Tommaso jumped on it and pedaled away.

CHAPTER 26

▼

Tom just sat there as if in a nightmare. A nightmare that tells you to strike the intruder but a strong and eerie force holds you down.

Then an inner voice spoke to him. 'Come on Tom you can do it. You did it before! You were only fifteen, remember? You took the bike back from the trespasser. The bike belonged to you!. This man is also a trespasser. He belongs in jail'!

The courageous short moment was quickly absorbed by unspoken words of fear and doubts, while the sweat smarted his eyes. At the attempt to wipe it off with the back of his hand, Peter warned him, "don't you fucking move!" rattling the gun under the table that sent sounds to Tom's ears like the thunder that follows the lightning that strikes the ground a yard away.

Dan and Jim shut off the sirens as they entered the strip and drove slowly searching every restaurant, every café.

"Park the car!" Jim said. "This is not working. We must walk. We'll split. I walk along the building side, you'll walk across by the seaside without losing sight of each other!"

"Yah!" Dan agreed.

Meanwhile Gianni and Phil, after delivery of Joni in the hands of two Uniforms with the warning 'keep your eyes on her at all time', drove to South Beach to sort of create a back up to the other two detectives. It was in the opening. By then every policeman on duty that day knew what was happening. Eight of them were ordered, two per each car to follow Phil and Gianni at an unsuspecting distance. After taking Joni into custody, the chief and the captain drove together, keeping the car at a comfortable distance from all of them.

The look of worry on the captain's face gave the chief incentive to complain.

"You know…well, I know you have a habit of shielding that crazy I-Italian, but I must administer him some restrains…"

"For God's sake, Chief," he responded addressing him officially. "He's on a job, his life is in jeopardy and you make statements like that?"

"Okay! But why can't he follow rules?"

"Because sometimes he doesn't give a fuck about them and neither do I. Why, do criminals follow rules? We have our ass daily exposed at the mercy of those assholes and when we have a hunch…well when we have a hunch we don't give a fuck about rules. One moment of distraction, a second of hesitation, could mean loss of lives, our life! Let me remind you, I was a lieutenant once. Like Tom, when my ass was exposed, I only followed my own instinct."

"Okay! I didn't mean to get you all agitated…"

"Chief! I like Tom, but that's beside the point at this moment. My concern is about his life. He may very well be a crazy I-Italian like you say, but he is the best…and another thing chief…"

"…And stop calling me chief. What is all this formality all of a sudden?"

"Because I'm angry and worried and you're pestering me with all these rules and regulations."

"Goddamned! You two come from the same screwed up Academy!" thus the chief rested his peace.

The captain also remained quiet as he drove full speed to South Beach. Then an ironic smile appeared on his lips as he thought, "Wait until *Miami Vise* gets on your ass for cutting into its territory!"

"What are you smiling at?"

"At life!" He answered grinning again.

CHAPTER 27

▼

Fear had plunged Tom into a state of impotency. Numbed he sat, incapable of commanding his body to act. Then he heard his inner voice again, but this time in a scolding manner.

"When did you become a coward?"

The answer, "When the rattling of the gun under the table that still sent a cacophonous reverberation in my ears, like thunder that follows the lightning that strikes the ground a yard away. That's when! And from the very moment my testicles were exposed at gunpoint at close range! That is also when I became a coward."

"Does that answer all the questions why one becomes a coward, Lieutenant SanTommaso?" The inner dialogue was now completed.

His fear totally exhausted the energetic flow of force in his body while his mind navigated with difficulty in an occult motivation of his senses. Then his brain clicked. Unstable under the present circumstance, but it clicked. Signs and vibes of reception from the academy's training that instructed survival under stress and fear during life threatening situations gave their response. Quickly the previous inertia disappeared, and with renewed vigor he proffered, "By the way, Paul sends you his love!"

"Paul? Paul!" What about Paul…"

"…Paul! You know, your half brother!"

"I see! You've done your homework."

"Yeah! I was good in school, not like spoiled brats of rich parents, like yourself and Paul," he said with confidence staring at Peter."

"Evidently you have a problem with rich spoiled brats. One more reason for me to eliminate you, this way you'll take your problem to your coffin. You'll never have to suffer again. Amen!" and again he rattled the gun under the table. This time, however, Tom remained calm and focused. Peter's continual rattling the gun under the table no longer gave him the sensation of thunders that follow the lightning that strikes the ground a yard away.

"Paul is in the can as an accomplice. I have personally booked him as your partner in crime. He admitted to be your half brother, which automatically makes him a prime suspect until proven otherwise. Tom really believed within the limits of confusion and doubt, that Paul was if not whole but half a perpetrator. "I've personally booked him!" he repeated. "I've personally read him his fucking rights, before I came looking for you," he continued strongly, showing no sign of fear. Instead he deeply stared at him, and without blinking once he kept on talking, "By the same talking, Doctor Smith didn't give you away. Your nasty looking eyes, congenital to those of Paul, gave both of you away. Moreover the accent and the sound of your voices that both of you tried to camouflage gave you away also. Let doc go. He has nothing to do with you or me. It's our battle! I want you and I'm going to get you one way or another. So let the man that made your face beautiful go! Doctor Smith was highly recommended to me from a cubano kid's sister. When I saw her, after Doctor Smith beautified her I got impressed. He cut, pulled, removed a few extra bones here and there and then stitched her into a new woman. Thus he successfully created out of an ugly pussy a beautiful girl. I knew her looks of old and I would not have touched her with your dick!"

He laughed so hard he almost took the doctor along.

But the doctor faintly smiled after making sure Peter was not looking towards him.

"See Peter…" he continued unperturbed in charge of what he called 'my fucked up sarcasm and arrogance.' "My interest in the doctor was solely to have him change my *'Greco Romano'* nose. I'm tired of looking at myself. Tired of the same old Italian Provincial face!"

Time, he was buying time with all that nonsensical talk. Furthermore, he was hoping to unbalance and confuse Peter, which seemed to be working.

Tom now had him lost.

He no longer could figure out what was going on.

"Insane, the motherfucker is insane!" he seemed to think. Then he looked over and beyond Tom with dead eyes like those of a dead fish.

When he snapped, on his face appeared to have a nasty tic that he could not control, which he quickly covered with his free hand.

Tom, sitting across from him couldn't help thinking about his own insanity, the insanity to hunt a killer without the help of his skilled detectives. And he wished that just this one time, Dan would ignore his duty to comply, seize the moment, and come to assist him. No! Dan would not disobey. Orders were orders to him! He would not budge!

Meanwhile he procrastinated in search of new arguments. But a sudden fear that Peter would get fed up with his nonsense and endanger the doctor, gave him a churning stomach and severe pains sat in his chest.

He frowned in restlessness.

The images of Dan and the gang insistently appeared as in a mirage.

No! He was alone on this. Right or wrong it had been his own stubbornness to pursue Peter alone. And if that would be no survival for him, out of this, he and only he, was the sole maker of it. Now with his forehead dropping sweat on the edge of the table, he hoped that something, perhaps a miracle would come to his aid. Thus, again impaled on his chair he felt; inept to start any physical action. He must depend again on the use of words. It was working for the time being. He must move on.

He focused again.

"Let the doctor go! I'm the one to whom you should concentrate all of your resources, not Doctor Smith."

Tom's past hesitation gave Peter time to refurbish.

"I have plenty of resources and plenty of ideas left. And I'm going to use them on both of you!" Peter said as if snapping out of a coma. Then he hurled a furious look that spread terror and horror, which affected the doctor if not Tom.

"You will need doctor Smith again, and soon." Tom responded with vigorous renovated energy ignoring the hate his eyes radiated. "Your face is deteriorating, a tic here and a tic there. It's going to collapse. Doc, here, can make you a new one again. Cut a nerve here and a nerve there and wipe out those nasty tics of yours. Let him go! I'll cut you a deal."

"Yes! I'll cut you a deal." He said again with hesitation.

"Yeah!" he continued for he knew that criminals liked the system of cutting deals. In the past, cutting deals had enabled many criminals to avoid going to the chair. "I have never known a judge to go back on his word. Come on Peter let's make a deal? Better yet, you have the right to any lawyer and with your money you can buy the best. One of those superstar lawyers can make you walk free. It's happening all the time lately."

Tom kept looking at him to see if any sign in Peter's eyes would reveal his thinking. There was some ostentation, but nothing cleared Tom's doubts that the criminal at the end of all that talking would have his way. And his way meant death.

Then, as for a pure miracle of God, Tom retracted fears and doubts that were in him before, and that by reflection, it seemed, were in Peter now.

Frustration and anger dwelled inside of him. He adjusted to his chair to camouflage a sudden sequence of uncontrollable tics. Then smiled a wounded smile to wipe them off. Tom read it as a clear sign of a precocious forthcoming of his face's disfiguration. An alert! The life expectancy of the plastic surgery was over. His face was already creasing.

"Go!" he said directly looking at the doctor. "I have no use for you!"

"Go!" said Tom softly watching Peter for any change in his moods.

The doctor sat in silent fear. His knees, stiff from the long sitting, creaked with pain as he slowly got up. He looked at both of them, in no way capable of muttering a word. He hesitated. Then slowly and undecided he nodded his head while backing up from his chair. Lamely he drifted away holding his briefcase.

"Not so fast, you! Leave the briefcase," Peter urged him.

"Put it on the table," Tom quickly said with a tone of command, just in case fuss was about to be raised.

"Okay," he said with a faint murmur and put it on the table. Then confused and fearful he turned his back on them again, and faltering, walked away. He stepped down, holding the handrail longside the few stairs that led to the sidewalk while having an inkling of being riddled with bullets across his torso. His heart suddenly beat violently and growled, as the wheels of locomotives on rails. Tom followed him with his eyes till he disappeared amidst the crowd.

One on one! There was no more time left for words or any more nonsense. It was time to act. The doctor gone gave Tom a new impulse. Intensely he looked at Peter while sharpening his ears. He tuned in on Peter's hand holding the pistol under the table, hoping to perceive even a slight thud. There was no more time left for indecision. Indeed, certain he was, that Peter was going to pull the trigger at any moment. And surely at that close range it would be impossible to miss. Instantly the abrupt pain on his testicles found its way to his abdomen. As if in a nightmare, the vision of the impact of the shot felt real and real looked the bits of his groins gone with the wind.

"Act!" he said within himself as if scolding himself. What happened to your motivation? Now, act now! Live this day as if there's no tomorrow! Your seconds are numbered!"

Thus suddenly depending solely on his gut feeling and luck, he took a deep breath and decided to live that moment as if tomorrow didn't exist. Against all odds, he delivered a powerful kick under the table that caught Peter's wrist.

The pistol fell on the ground.

Swirled. Exploded.

The projectile found its way to the table's leg, ripped out a sliver that infiltrated Tom's calf and sent him backwards to the ground.

At the sound of the blast, the people that were promenading on the strip, and from inside the restaurant, seized by fear, ran in all directions. They pushed each other and trampled on children in the attempt to look for shelter. Peter quickly located the gun, picked it up and pulled on the trigger. Jammed, he hurled it on Tom's head.

He snapped the briefcase from the table and hastily walked away. He crossed the above ground platform and jumped off the three wooden steps that led to the sidewalk. He pushed and knocked down everyone that either intentionally or unaware, obstructed him from running towards the shore.

Meanwhile, Tom, coming back to his senses after being stunned from the gun, which caused a deep laceration on his head, slowly got up. He tried to block with some tissues found on the floor, the rivulets of blood coming from his calf and his head.

"Police!" he warned, flagging his badge to the waiters and patrons that still were franticly, coming out the restaurant.

"Police! Stay back, down, down, on the floor, cover your head! You! Get down now!" he shouted to a man who stood up near him.

"He crossed the street and he took to the shore," the man whispered while he was getting on his knees to get down.

"Thanks," Tom said. "Stay down! Cover your head!" Then with a lame leg and his head in pain, he followed the directions given by the man. Quite a distance away and out of his gun's range, there was Peter, still carrying the briefcase.

Tom shouted, "Freeze!" In vain, Peter kept on running.

The sting from his calf, and the contusion on his head, still bleeding, made its weight felt but Tom refused to abandon the chase.

Dan and Jim saw and heard the commotion from a block or two up. They quickly ran and met at the scene. They were told the direction the two men had taken.

"The officer is wounded!" a voice rose from the crowd.

Dan radioed the captain and the chief. "Tom is wounded but we don't know the condition of his health as of now, however we have located him. He's chasing Peter. We are on our way!" Then still following the chase with Jim nearby, he relayed the message to the troopers and in full command told them, "Shut the sirens and slowly patrol the seaside between

13th and 20th St.. Stay alert and wait for orders. Do not! Absolutely do not follow the chase!"

Phil and Gianni were told to park the car. "Walk the beat southbound!"

Tom was loosing ground on Peter but didn't quit! Time to time he would stop to warn Peter to freeze, but mostly did it to catch his breath. He was too far from Tom's gun's range. The wounded leg was giving up, his panting unbearable.

Meanwhile Peter changed direction. He trailed a beach attendant on a dune buggy driving slowly in oblivion scouting the beach. Tom knew that if Peter reached the buggy and succeeded to get possession of it, it meant the end of the chase. He put all his effort on waiving and shouting hoping to get the motorist's attention. It was in vain, for the boy kept his speed minding his own business seeing no harm in two men jogging. As Peter got within reach of the buggy he threw the briefcase in. With both hands he grabbed the back bar of the vehicle and jumped in. He picked the brief-case up and slammed it on the boy's head. The fellow wobbled. The blow stunned him but he was capable of holding on to the steering wheel. With a clear head now, he hastily, smartly and skillfully maneuvered his vehicle at full speed. Then he zigzagged it to unbalance the perpetrator. Peter anticipated the boy's intentions, dropped the briefcase and furiously threw a sequence of punches at him. That didn't intimidate the boy at all who aggressively responded to the attack. However, feeling he was losing the battle, he suddenly jammed on the brakes. The sudden stop unbalanced Peter but he managed to hold on the back bar. The boy pressed heavily on the accelerator and then jammed on the brakes again bringing the buggy to a full stop. They both vacillated but both failed to plummet by holding on each other's arms. As they reached stability, they reciprocally delivered a sequence of conflicting punches on each other face and stomach. The brawl favored the boy, when with a lucky upright punch he caught the aggressor between the Adam's apple and the chin. Peter fell to the ground. His body bounced and rolled like a log on a river's strong current then stopped in a ditch of sand. He staggered as he tried to get on his feet.

Shaken and stressed out he picked up the briefcase that the boy had thrown at his head and started to run again.

Tom quickly seized the moment and dragging his lame leg along he shouted flagging his badge. Finally, he got the young man's attention.

The boy promptly delivered the buggy.

"Thanks! Get out of the area, take shelter!" he said furiously panting while he took possession of the vehicle. Depending solely on a new but short renewed vigor, he quickly put it in gear and drove towards Peter gaining a new momentum. It had been a long day for Tom and a scary one as well. The fatigue from the chase and the wounds, still bleeding, had depleted his endurance. His eyes suddenly blurred. Peter became a distant faded figure, a running earthly ghost. He shook his head, came to his senses again and the running earthly ghost reappeared in his former form, however slow in his movements.

"Freeze!" Tom shouted as he was closing in, hoping not to blur again, "Freeze! Freeze you sonofabitch!"

But Peter kept on going. His running was now a mere walk. He dragged his feet along while holding, with one hand his abdomen and the other the briefcase. The rumbling of a mufflers closing in on him, Peter looked back to check the distance and, appearing closer than he thought, he tried to run faster. Unsuccessfully, however, for his strength was gone, and pains tormented his stomach.

It was now time for Tom to put faith in all of his boot camp training. He jumped out of the vehicle letting it run loose, pointed the gun and shouted," Freeze or I'll blow your head off."

Peter didn't turn or stop. He kept on heaving his feet along, still holding his lower abdomen with one hand and the briefcase with the other.

He felt lost.

But Tom was not in any better shape. Again his eyes blurred and again although closer now, Peter appeared as a walking earthly ghost. Tom shook his head. The fog in his eyes cleared. He knelt on his good leg, held the gun with both hands and shot a sequence of shots all around him without hitting. "Freeze bastard! The next bullet," he shouted again, "It's your skull."

Peter believed him, stopped and turned to face Tom.

"Don't move! Get down on your face, put your hands over your head!"

In response to Peter's hesitation, Tom still kneeling in the shooting position pulled the trigger and with a sequence of shots, blew away part of the briefcase. The legal tender waived in the air like feathers.

Peter fell on his knees and dropped whatever was left of the briefcase, still dishing out dollars that danced away waving in the wind as if in a choreographic ballet. With both hands he held his stomach, his eyes out of orbit in convulsion as a wounded defeated animal while a sequence of tics tormented his face.

"On your stomach, put your hands over your head. It's the final warning Peter!"

Peter fell sprawled supine.

Tom walked slowly pulling on his lame leg, "Turn on your stomach!" he commanded. Peter tried to comply but his strength had forsaken him. Tom lamely drew closer, put his hands behind his back lifted him and rolled him over. Grasping his wrists, he twisted them behind Peter's back to handcuff him. He didn't have them on him or he'd lost them during the chase. He pinned his lower spine with his knee. Then quickly, he pressed the muzzle of his gun on Peter's neck. Then without haste albeit furiously panting, he read him his rights.

"You have...the fucking...right to remain silent. Have the right to hire...a lawyer. Every...every fucking...word you say can be...used against you in the fucking court...court of law..."

Worn out, with difficulty keeping his head up, Tom was still mumbling over Peter's rights when Dan and Jim reached them. Then within seconds the troopers and the ambulance were at the site.

Dan quickly took the gun away from him just in case Tom loaded with adrenaline, would pull the trigger and blow Peter's head off.

Then as Jim handcuffed Peter, Dan knelt down next to Tom and said, "Lieutenant St. Thomas, it's all over, sir! It is all over!"

Tom tried to look at him. His eyes blurred and passed out.

Dan called Maria while the ambulance took Tom to the emergency room. He told her quickly what had happened and offered to take her to the hospital if she would meet him at Bayside's main entrance.

Maria burst into tears when she met Dan. To calm her down he said, "a few scratches, Maria, really, a few scratches. He's fine. They're running a few tests because of a little loss of blood. He's under observation now. Leave your car here. I'll have an officer drive it to your door before morning!"

When Tom opened his eyes, although still drowsy, he saw Maria sitting on a chair next to his bed, sobbing. He attempted a smile and murmured, "So, why are you crying? It's not that I am dead. Here lean over."

With the corner of his sheet he tried to wipe her tears, but never made it to her eyes. The sheet dropped off his hand and he fell into the deepest sleep.

CHAPTER 28

It was five in the morning when Tom woke up. He raised his eyes to Maria. She was dozing on the chair. "This woman's going to drive me crazy," he murmured, then smiling he thought, "Doesn't miss a shot!"

Awakened by Tom rustling on the bed, Maria opened her eyes and smiled at him. He nodded his head, frowned and scolded her, "What was the reason for you to stay up watching over me? Don't you have work to do at home?"

"Shut up," she said. "Is it possible that even dead you have to be nasty!" Thus she got up bent over him and kissed him. He absorbed it, smiled and murmured, "I love you!"

"What're you doing?" Painstakingly she asked, as he tried to get up. "Stay in bed. They haven't released you!"

"Release my ass. Help me get dressed…"

Maria's complaints didn't get far.

"Maria, be a good girl! We have to get the fuck out of here. I'm allergic to the hospital's nasty smell of medicine."

Maria had anticipated he might be in need of clothes. Since she knew that Tom would not change his mind about tiptoeing out of the giant building, permission or no permission, she bent down to pick the small suitcase up. He looked at her curvaceous behind. He smiled. He stretched his hand and pinched her.

"Oh," she jumped, "we're not in Italy here!"

"Have we ever made love in a hospital bed?"

"Oh no, let's get out of here," she promptly responded with frowns, albeit she felt the rush of her arousal. "Oh no, let's get the hell out of here!"

"Pave the way for me. Check the corridor and the nurses' counter. If they're scratching their ass we'll walk out nonchalantly and as smoothly as motherfuckers...

"I don't see how you think we're going to make it with you limping and with me totally lost in this labyrinth..."

"Next time I fall in love with a woman she better be a deaf mute!"

"Would be no next time, I'll kill you first!"

They made it outside.

They steered clear. Tom hanging on to her to make his walking less painful. Then he suddenly stopped.

"What now?" The sudden stop unbalanced Maria and tripped off holding on him.

"Wait!" he said.

"Stay here, I have to attend to some small business!" he said attempting a smile. Then lamely walked towards a figure that was playing hide and seek behind a three.

"Al Pacino, come out of there!"

Jose' with his usual nonchalant gait, walked towards Tom, smiled and said, "Man! Lieutenant you're a crazy fuck! A real crazy fuck..."

Tom attempted a laugh, drifted towards the boy, looked at him with a smirk and proffered, "You're a crazier fuck than I could ever be, Mr. Al Pacino." Then he turned to Maria who was reaching him and asked, "Maria honey...can I borrow fifty dollars?"

"Hey, hey, man? What you're doing? I refuse! You're offending me, man. I did you a favor. You don't pay someone that does you a favor."

"You're my idol José!" Tom attempted again to laugh. "I'm sure I will need to summon you up one of this days...all kidding aside. Thanks, I owe you one. I must go! God speed my friend!"

He left holding onto Maria.

José looked towards them as they departed shaking his head.

"Hey…see you around okay!

"Yes! See you around!"

The next day, Maria stood by him and watched over him just in case he tried to sneak out to go to work. And there came a time, during the day, when he almost did tiptoe out like a punished child that finds satisfaction breaking the rules. She caught him in the act. She scolded him and slapped him on the wrist just like one does with a child.

"You're a snake…Get to bed! It's an order!"

However, the following day she was not capable or convincing enough to contain him.

He went to work.

He hobbled along the corridor on the way to the chief's office. All the Uniforms around, clapped their hands as soon as they saw him, and murmured words of praise. He smiled and waved in rebuff his hands, murmuring, "Oh shut up all of you."

"Good morning, Tom, come in," said the chief when he saw Tom peeping in. "Come in," he continued getting up to meet him, offering his assistance.

"What's all this sympathy?" Tom said refusing the chief's help. "Seems I should get wounded more often. Perhaps you'll treat me more humanly," he continued with a smile.

"Sit down! You're impossible. I'm going to show you that I am capable of liking you. In fact I'm giving you two weeks off, with pay of course!"

"Thank you, but I have a few things I have to finish first!"

"It's an order Tom!"

"I'm not disputing it! But I really have a few things I have to finish."

"Get the hell out of here, I must get ready for TV's interviews and I'm late."

Tom slowly got up and lamely drifted to the exit.

"Oh by the way Tom? If at all possible, do you think? Perhaps, I can borrow one of your suits?"

"I'll have Dan deliver a few of them, you take your pick…however…"

"…What?" the chief worried, quickly asked him.

"Afterwards you have to take it to my drycleaner…"

"Of course! That goes without saying! What do you think I'm a swine?"

"I mean, not any drycleaner, the one I'm a patron of. Must be that one!"

"So? Why, I understand…"

"They charge twenty five dollars per suit!"

"Golly…holly cow!"

Now, out of the chief's office, everything looked normal. Loren was now at her desk. He, as a matter of fact, saluted her by knocking his knuckles on the desk. Startled, she looked up with worry on her face and whispered, "Tom, God! Are you okay?" while tears started to build up on her eyes.

"Hey, hey, here wipe your tears," he said handing her a tissue. "In our line of work we have no time for tears…" Then smiling he caressed her hair and jokingly continued, "If I were not half married I'd take you away from your boyfriend…"

"Is he going to be okay?"

"Clean! He's clean! I must run!"

Jim was already in his wired-room and Gianni and Phil were out looking for—*ladri di galline*—chickens' thieves.

Dan was in charge of bringing Paul to see him. And he did.

He walked into Tom's office with Paul cuffed as if he were a criminal.

"Take those cuffs off, Dan," he murmured with a faint smile and a smirk of disapproval on his face. "Leave us alone! Please."

"You knew it," he said to Paul. You knew he was a killer and that he'd committed those crimes."

"Lieutenant, you should be in bed recuperating. From what I see and if the rumors around this station are accurate, you've been severely wounded…"

"…Thank you for your concern," Tom cut in. "But as of this moment you'll answer my questions straight forward, omitting the usual nonsense! Is that clear?"

"As clear as a night embroidered with stars!"

"And skip the poetry!"

"Okay," he continued ignoring Tom's smirk. Peter and I are not, half brothers, not stepbrothers either, we're twins..."

"...Twins?"

"Yeah! Twins! We were conceived in the same moment and nurtured in the same womb for nine months before delivery. We're identical twins but, not identical at all, accept for our physical resemblance."

"And that was the giveaway!" Tom said.

"At any rate, Peter, his real name, like Paul's mine..."

"What is the real last name of these two splendid spoiled brats of rich parents?" Again he caught himself on his short psycho trip about spoiled brats of rich parents.

"Dubois! As you already know! I changed my name to Invisible, for disguise, of course."

"Why did he have to kill for money if..."

"Lieutenant may I keep going before I change my mind, get out of here and take legal action against you and this agency for embezzlement, and captivity of an innocent man. You have taken too much of my time thus postponing the joys of a rich pauper's peaceful life..."

"Spare me! Go on!"

"My parents are dead. They died on the scene, in an automobile accident and when Peter found out he was not the half beneficiary of the will, he went into convulsions."

"Wound you?"

"All his life he had done nothing but squander their money, pretending it all..." Paul continued ignoring Tom's interruption. "Never! He gave them the benefit of his love. On the contrary, he mistreated and abused them, sometimes at gunpoint. He never gave them a moment of peace. I, if you will, and without any effort on my part, became the apple of their eyes."

Tom did not mutter a word now. Instead, he just listened shaking his head time to time, but believing every word Paul said.

"When I went to the lawyer's office for the reading of the will, I expected to meet Peter there. I waited for him to show up while the lawyer was adjusting and laying the papers out. As he start reading I asked, 'shouldn't we wait for by brother?'"

"According to what I have here there's no mention of a brother!"

"I was willing to support him, to make him comfortable and put him on a fund for life. When I talked to him about it, he refused to listen. Stormed out of the house. We both used to live at home with our parents. I'd never seen him again until I saw the clips in the Alabama Chronicle. And…and then I saw him a month ago or so!"

"A month ago? How, where?"

"I mean he saw us, stalked us, you may say. He watched us from his car while we walked to John G's the day we went for lunch there. He knew who you were. When you and I split he came to talk to me…"

"This is getting fascinating. And you told him that I had contacted Doctor Smith…"

"…Doctor Smith? I knew nothing about doctor Smith. He's been watching every movement you made since your first day at BBPD. That day when he came to see me, he appeared very nervous. In fact a nervous wreck! He had trailed you down to Miami and saw you talking to that doctor…Doctor Smith was and still is a total stranger to me…"

"Why didn't you come clean with me? When he found out I was after him, why didn't you tell me? You were linked, why didn't you tell me. I could…you could have spared me a lot of indecision!"

"Would you? Perhaps, perhaps knowing you, I had a hunch you were connected…spare me the agony to betray him. Betraying my only brother, my twin brother was not in any of my childhood dreams come true. Perhaps I should have given you a hint or two…"

"You should have told me! As a citizen of this country you had the sacrosanct obligation to do so. Brother or no brother. And save me a lot of sleepless nights."

"It is my brother you're talking about, my twin…"

"The law, Paul, is specific about reporting a crime, no matter what! You failed to do your duty! Besides, you have mislead me with all your bullshit. You have willingly deceived me!"

"It's easy for you to say," he answered omitting the last part of Tom's argument. "However, if you didn't succeed, I was prepared to come clean and give you some tips. I'm sorry! I couldn't do it. Not straight forward!"

Tom stood in silence and was motionless accept for a shake of his head from time to time, showing no approval or disapproval while Paul was in vain to empty the whole sack. Then suddenly, Tom rose his eyes over the brim of his glasses and asked, "How much did you inherit, may I at least know…"

"Nine million in cash plus the compound we all were living in and a bunch of other properties and stocks" Paul said while Tom totally closed his eyelids over his eyes. Then his mouth dropped open so much, he could have swallowed his desk.

When Tom finally digested the indigestible amount of Paul's dowry, he murmured, "He killed to get even patrimony! He could have killed you and gotten the dough, plus the properties no?"

"He could have, I make him capable, but he had a hunch that the money was in a safe place! And as far as the rest of the assets, he had no knowledge or concept of any of it.

"The money, of course, is accumulating interest in Switzerland's banks?"

"You do your own math…!

"Why don't you adopt me?" Tom said with a smile.

Peter didn't answer him but smiled with him going into deep silence dropping his chin over his chest. With tears in his eyes he then looked at Tom and with a thread of voice, asked.

"What's going to happen to him?"

"The DA will probably go for Capital Punishment."

"And of course, that will make you happy?"

"Not necessarily!" He stated.

"Why not! You're the law! That is what satisfies your ego!"

Tom smiled a sad smile. He nodded his head a few times then without second thought exclaimed "Wrong! The Capital Punishment or death penalty is a barbaric law! I'll never understand why, in a country as civilized as ours, it still exists!"

"Why then…"

"Paul, I don't write the law! I execute it! My job is done the moment I read the criminals their rights!"

978-0-595-35111-4
0-595-35111-5

Printed in the United States
31068LVS00002B/304-330

9 780595 351114